The Snowman Maker

"When love takes you in its arms,
You know you've made it Home."
The Snowman Maker

The Snowman Maker

Barbara Briggs Ward

The Snowman Maker

Published by Wheatmark®
1760 East River Road, Suite 145
Tucson, Arizona 85718 USA
www.wheatmark.com

In cooperation with:
The Maggie O'Shea Company
P.O. Box 627
Ogdensburg, New York 13669 U.S.A.
www.barbarabriggsward.com

ISBN: 978-1-60494-901-8 (paperback)
ISBN: 978-1-60494-902-5 (ebook)
LCCN: 2012950287

rev201301

Chapter One

THE TRAIN WAS LATE DUE TO a blizzard disrupting holiday travel all along the East Coast. Ellie didn't mind waiting. It gave her time to get her thoughts together. Over their almost thirty-nine years of marriage rarely had she and Ben had problems communicating, but that changed after his father died. Ben seemed distant now. His father had been ill for quite some time so it wasn't as if his passing had been out of the blue. Ellie had mentioned getting the tree over the coming weekend but Ben didn't seem interested. He claimed he needed to catch up after having spent the last few months working nonstop with a major client.

"A project like that doesn't come along every day. I needed to give it my full attention."

"No problem," she'd told him over the phone the night before as she remembered all the Christmases when he'd been the one chopping down the tree and dragging it out of the woods. "I'll wait for Andy to get home. He can go with me."

Even though she'd volunteered their twenty-two-year-old, there was no guarantee he'd go. It had been a hard semester. He'd waited before going on to school, but now he was talking about quitting.

"Why waste money if I'm clueless?" he'd question. "I don't need a degree to get a job."

Ellie tried pointing out the difference between a job and a career but her words fell on deaf ears.

Daughter Maggie chose her career by age ten after getting into the few cosmetics Ellie kept in a bathroom drawer. She loved all the colors. She even loved the plastic cases they came in. After earning her degree, she was hired by a major leader in the beauty industry, garnering praise as she climbed the ladder. Since Maggie was working in London, it'd be only Ellie, Andy, and Ben in the old stone home for Christmas. Ellie was not looking forward to the holidays.

A SUDDEN BUSTLE ALERTED ELLIE. BEN'S train was approaching. Instead of anticipating his stepping onto the platform as she'd done so many times before, she felt a nervousness she had never thought possible when it came to their relationship. Ellie couldn't put her finger on it. Had he grown tired of her? She'd gone right into nursing following high school, working her way up from floor nurse to supervisor. In a few years she'd be retiring. While she was aware that Ben was surrounded by more exciting, fit women who were ready to do what was necessary to get what they wanted, walking remained Ellie's only exercise, and pulling her hair back in a French twist had been the extent of her hairstyling. Her idea of a spa was getting her grays covered every five weeks or so.

"You should join a gym," Maggie often suggested.

Ellie admired this younger generation of women. They were aware. They were driven to achieve and have it all, even more so than the bra-burning women Ellie remembered watching on a black-and-white TV screen.

At times, when lying next to Ben with the clock ticking on the bedroom mantel, Ellie would think back to when she'd put advancement at the hospital on hold when the kids were little.

"I don't want to discourage her," she'd rationalize, "but in the real world, you can't have it all. In the real world, something has to give."

"She'll learn," Ben would say. "She has her own path to follow."

DESPITE WHATEVER WAS BOTHERING BEN, THE sight of him edging his way through the crowd made Ellie's heart quicken. He still had that dimple on his left cheek. His smile was still the teasing smile that had melted her into mush the first time he had visited her older brother, Paul, back when they were all in high school. After that, he was at their house almost every day. Ben thought of Ellie as Paul's little sister until he saw her in a bathing suit, slathered in baby oil, lying in the sun next to her two best friends. He'd tried getting her attention that day, but the girls had the music blasting. A few years later, Ben made his move.

THERE WAS SOMETHING ABOUT HIM IN the midst of all those strangers and the trains coming and going. He had a sense of himself. He wasn't your average nine-to-fiver. Fussing over her scarf and straightening her camel coat, Ellie braced for whatever mood he might be in. As passengers overloaded with gifts rushed to open arms, Ellie's thoughts went back to another holiday season when Maggie was seven or eight. She'd been sick for a good week. The doctor had told Ellie to keep her calm, so on Christmas morning Maggie was resting on the sofa. But when her father started to open the gift she and Andy had given him, Maggie sat straight up as he ripped the paper off and pulled out a large container of Lincoln Logs. From his reaction, it was obvious he was pleased. The idea for the gift came one night during a dinner conversation about favorite Christmas presents. That's when he told the kids his favorite gift ever had been a can of those logs, but he couldn't remember whatever happened to it.

"I loved building things, even when I was a kid," recalled the successful architect. "I remember doing simple drawings on paper. Then I'd try building them with my Lincoln Logs. When I put those red plastic chimneys on, I felt as if I'd built the Empire State Building."

WATCHING BEN HELP A WOMAN WITH her luggage, Ellie was certain he'd already left his mark, even if it wasn't the Empire State Building. With a hint of a beard and wearing the tweed jacket she felt brought out his deep brown eyes, Ben soon greeted Ellie with a simple hug and "How's traffic?"

"Not bad, considering the number of shoppers out despite this snow storm."

"Is dinner ready, or should we stop?"

"Dinner's ready. Your favorite," she replied.

On the way home, he fell asleep. Getting off at their exit, Ellie paused for oncoming traffic. With the signal light ticking in rhythm to windshield wipers humming and snow falling, Ellie looked over at Ben who was curled up with his head against the window. Tears came from nowhere.

"Where have you gone, my love?" she whispered in the silence of a winter's night. "Where have you gone?"

Chapter Two

In the morning light, winter's wrath could be seen everywhere. Snow drifts defined the sides of roads plowed into the wee hours. Looking out the back window, Ellie couldn't tell where their property line ended and the neighbor's began. It was hard enough to see where the hedgerow had been on a clear day after Ben spent a good part of the fall clearing it out. With the help of Henry, the old man he called on whenever he needed an extra set of hands, Ben had built a stone wall in its place. In the spring they planned on doing the same to the front of the property. They'd already cleared away the brush. It didn't matter to Ben what he was building, as long as he was creating.

"These stone homes are beauties," Henry often remarked, "but they require constant upkeep."

Henry knew everyone. He knew family histories. He sometimes knew more about families than the families themselves. He lived a few miles down the road in his own stone homestead. It'd been a working farm until his wife passed away some ten years back. While Henry had kept a few horses, he'd sold almost everything in the barn when Helen died, including the bells he'd used when taking orphans for sleigh rides. After every one of those sleigh rides, Helen would serve the boys and girls her sugar cookies with hot chocolate. Henry and Helen never had children of their own.

It was an accident during a blizzard close to Christmas a few years after losing her that brought Henry back around. Half asleep in his chair, he'd heard a noise through the storm. Henry knew it meant someone had gone off the road. He knew it had been in front of the granary where the road took a sharp turn. Henry didn't hesitate. He made his way through the snowdrifts and into the barn—the very place he'd ignored since Helen's passing. But that night, as the wind shook the rafters, Henry found Helen's spirit embracing him as he grabbed flashlights and blankets and assisted a young man who was more frightened than anything. Once Henry got him inside the barn, they talked while waiting for the storm to pass. It turned out the young man was on his way home for the holidays. He'd heard of Henry from his uncle, who had been an orphan and once a passenger in Henry's sleigh. That night, the sleigh was back out again.

"Roads are buried," Henry told him. "This is the only way to get you home to your family."

With the horses hitched up and blankets on board, Henry loaded the young man into the sleigh and took off through the back fields. Though the sleigh bells were missing, that act of kindness brought Henry back to life.

After getting home from the train station the night before, Ellie had again confronted Ben as they sat down to eat. She knew he was tired. She knew she shouldn't, but she did.

"This is getting a little old, Ellie. You have to accept what I tell you. I have a lot on my mind."

Ellie couldn't drop it. Down deep, she felt as if she was losing him.

"This is foreign to me, Ben. You're shutting me out. We've always worked through whatever life has thrown at us." By then, the tears were back. "If there's someone else, please have the decency to tell me. You owe me that, Ben."

She kept telling herself to stay strong, but the hole in her heart didn't hear. Neither did Ben. He was out of the kitchen and on his way to bed.

Today, with the sun warming her tired eyes, Ellie was determined to make this new day a good one. She vowed not to bring up that topic again, at least not while Andy was home. Knowing them as well as he did, Andy would pick up on the tension right away. He had enough problems of his own. He didn't need another worry on his plate, and Ellie certainly didn't want to ruin what she and Ben still had, although she didn't know what that was anymore. She had to believe what Ben was telling her. She knew no other way.

One thing was for certain: Andy would be home late that afternoon. When he called, Ellie mentioned getting a tree. He seemed okay with it. Between the two of them, Ellie felt like she was walking on egg shells and that was not how it was supposed to be at Christmastime.

"I guess the perfect Christmas is in the movies," she told herself, pouring a cup of coffee.

Hearing Ben coming down the back stairs, Ellie took another mug out of the cupboard. This not knowing what to say to the man who'd been her only lover—the man who played the guitar like Hendrix—was unfamiliar territory. She'd never admit it but there were times when she missed the Ellie who'd worn flowers in her hair and would have gone to Woodstock with her long-haired, guitar-playing Ben, except for the fact that her parents wouldn't let her. Ellie always wondered what path their life together would have taken if his band could have played more than backup on that stage in the pouring rain. Fate has a way of stepping in. Ben made his mark with a different type of steel.

"Coffee?" she asked.

"Just a half cup."

"Toast? Bagel?"

"Nothing, thanks." Reaching for the milk, he added, "There is no other woman, Ellie."

That was all Ellie needed. Whatever it was, they would face it together. They'd managed to get through almost losing Maggie when she was fourteen and in a car accident with her best friend's mother. They'd survived a flood and an ice storm that knocked everything out for a good two weeks. They'd weathered the kids having one childhood ailment after another, plus Andy's broken arm and appendicitis. They'd stood firm when he wanted to drop out of high school. They'd worked with him to get his grades up. After holding down a job for a few years, he'd been accepted at a state college about an hour away. They felt he was set. Unfortunately, Ben and Ellie were facing a new battle—trying to keep him there after only one semester.

Chapter Three

"There's so much snow." Ben was looking out the back door. "It'll be tough picking out a tree."

That was Ben's first mention of Christmas. Ellie trod softly. "Maybe by tomorrow, some of it will have melted. They're calling for mid-thirties today."

"If need be, we might be able to go by sleigh."

"Henry's?"

"Yes, trusting he's able and willing."

The old man had more than one sleigh, so Ellie questioned, "The sleigh Andy called Santa's Christmas sleigh?"

"That's the one."

When Andy was little, Henry would sit him on his lap and tell him stories. Sometimes the stories were about a sleigh Henry called the Christmas sleigh.

"Why does Santa need another sleigh?" Andy would ask Henry.

"There are boys and girls he visits who don't have homes of their own. They live together in one big place, and Santa uses a special sleigh when he stops there on Christmas Eve."

"Why?"

"Santa brings the children more than toys," Henry would explain.

"What does he bring them?"

"He always brings boots and coats, shoes, and pajamas. And sometimes Santa brings a family."

Andy never understood what Henry meant by Santa bringing a family. Like most kids, Andy thought everyone had a family. Henry never pushed it. Not many knew how hard he and Helen worked helping the orphanage find families. Not many knew what it really meant to Henry—not even Helen.

The thought of going to the woods in a horse and sleigh in search of a tree gave Ellie hope. She'd always put her heart into creating a Christmas full of memories. She worried what memories would come of this Christmas fast approaching.

"I haven't been in a sleigh like that since I was a little girl. It might be what the three of us need."

"Maybe going after a Christmas tree is about more than the tree this year."

"We all lose our way at some point, Ben. You have the strength within you to move mountains."

"Spoken by my wife."

"Spoken by someone who knows you."

"Remember our first time, Ellie? I was thinking about that last night when I couldn't get to sleep. We do have a history, don't we?"

"We do."

"History's important. Knowing where you come from is important."

"What do you mean, Ben?"

"I'm just talking." Checking his watch, Ben grabbed his work coat hanging by the back door. "You didn't answer me, Ellie."

"Do you mean that rainy afternoon when I lost my virginity in your parents' cabin as they were tying up their canoe? Yes, I remember. That was the fastest I ever got dressed or made a bed. Even faster was how we jumped back in when they left, once the sun came back out."

Lingering by the door, Ben added, "I need some time, Ellie. It's good to be home."

Watching him shovel, Ellie felt they'd connected. She felt energized. They'd been together longer than she could remember. It was that history thing he touched on. They had it. They'd worked on it. As she watched him clean the snow off his truck, his words played back through her mind:

Knowing where you come from is important.

Ellie realized he was saying much more in that simple sentence. It remained to be seen what that was.

Chapter Four

Late afternoon had become early evening by the time Andy walked through the front door loaded down with duffle bags full of laundry and a backpack. He wasn't two steps in before he dropped it all in the hallway and headed to the refrigerator without acknowledging Ben dozing by the fireplace. One thing he did keep hold of was a guitar. He laid the worn case on the counter.

"Not even a hello?" said Ellie.

"I'm starving. I haven't eaten all day, Mom."

"Why so late? We were worried."

After pulling out a container of spaghetti and meatballs, Andy reached for the milk carton. Without answering his mother, he grabbed a plate and fork and sat down at the table.

"I can warm that up for you."

"I can't wait."

"You have the school meal program. Do you use it?"

"Not much. Food isn't any good."

Once he had his fleece off, Ellie could tell he'd lost weight. Making a cup of tea, Ellie sat down next to her son who used to love curling up next to her on the sofa in his pajamas. Most times he'd fall asleep before Ellie finished reading books chosen from shelves in the den. Pulling the blanket up around him, moving his baby-fine hair away from his eyes,

Ellie would stay put, especially when winter was at the windows. Ben never believed her when she'd tell him flannel pajamas could smell of frogs and snails and puppy-dog tails, but they did, when she and Andy were sitting on the old sofa with the wind trying to get in. They really did.

Now that baby-fine hair looked as though it hadn't seen a brush since the beginning of the semester after Ellie and Ben left him standing in the dorm room surrounded by others who didn't appear too happy to be there either. It was different when leaving Maggie. She wanted to be there. She'd defined her goal before arriving and went for it.

Andy reminded Ellie of Ben when he was Andy's age. All he cared about was his guitar. It was a conversation with Henry that gave Ben the idea of turning his curiosity about building into something solid. Once his curiosity was defined, the rest fell into place. He applied to school and never looked back. Between schools, he and Ellie married. They lived near campus, up on the third floor of an old brick building. Ben loved it there. He'd often stay up sketching what he would do with it if he owned it. Oddly enough, he bought the place once he opened his firm. When he completed its transformation, an article about it appeared in the *New York Times*. That was the first of several recognitions Ben would receive.

The location had been perfect for the young couple since bikes were their only means of transportation. Ellie was doing shift work at a nearby hospital, and more often than not, it was the midnight shift. In the wintertime she'd walk to the hospital. Getting a ride back was never a problem. In those early mornings when Ellie returned to the apartment, the two made love as the sun came up. Anticipation would build in every corner of that one-bedroom flat as Ben slowly unbuttoned her uniform. Slipping it down off her shoulders, he'd then pick Ellie up and carry her to their mattress on the floor where they never could get enough of each other. So many times Ben would rush out the door late for class, his hair as unruly as his son's, who'd finished his spaghetti and was about to cut himself a piece of apple pie when Ben walked into the kitchen.

"I didn't hear the front door open."

Andy was after ice cream. He didn't answer.

"What time did you get home? Your mother and I were worried."

It was Ellie who filled Ben in. An argument was something she wanted to avoid. She seemed to have had more patience when Maggie was Andy's age. Her mother might have been right when questioning her having a baby later in life, although labor had only been three hours long and Andy weighed a healthy eight pounds.

"Any chocolate sauce?"

"In the side door, Andy."

With his plate full, Andy sat back down.

"I see you brought your guitar home." Ben couldn't miss the case. He had one identical to it upstairs. "What are you playing?"

"Mostly Hendrix."

"Hendrix was your father's idol."

"I know, Mom."

Andy devoured his dessert while Ellie told him about their plans to go by sleigh to get the tree.

"Breakfast will be ready early," she added. "We don't want to make Henry wait."

"That old guy still driving his sleighs?"

"He certainly is, Andy," said Ben. "He looks forward to seeing you again."

"I don't think I'll go, Dad. I'm sleeping in."

"We'll need your help. You know how big the tree has to be, and Henry isn't as young as he thinks he is. But don't tell him that!"

"I'll see."

Grabbing hold of his guitar, Andy went upstairs. Ben wasn't far behind.

With the house quiet, Ellie worked around the kitchen. Between doing a few loads of Andy's wash, she brought down boxes of ornaments packed away in the front hall. Included was a small box marked SAVE FOR BEN/CHRISTMAS. Ben's father had given it to him shortly before he passed away. Ellie remembered how unsettled he was when returning home with it.

"It's as if Dad's given up, Ellie," Ben had explained. "I didn't want to take his stuff, but he looked so disappointed."

"It's more than stuff to your father, Ben. He's making sure it gets where he feels it needs to be. He's taking care of business while he can," Ellie had pointed out.

Ben put the box away with all the other Christmas decorations. Being an only child, he took care of his father's business after his death. Some of that business would prove life-changing.

Chapter Five

Ellie knew that if she went upstairs she'd only lie there thinking of what else she had to do, so she pulled the tree lights out of the boxes and plugged them in. She wanted to be sure they worked. Ben had no patience for stuff that didn't work when he needed it to work. Her plan was to have everything ready to go once the tree was secured in the same corner of the front room where Christmas trees always stood. To accommodate the mammoth pines, Ben had altered the room one summer, years back.

"Angled just so, the tree can be seen in all directions, inside the house and out," he'd explained to Ellie. Larger windows had been installed to make that happen while never losing the original layout or feel of the house.

After she'd checked the lights, Ellie sorted through decorations, putting them in piles. Some were good to go. Others were in need of attention. Then she took hold of the box marked Save for Ben/ Christmas. She knew he wouldn't mind if she opened it. She knew it'd be up to her anyway, even if Ben had been sitting there, so Ellie pulled back the crinkled tape and opened the box. Layers of yellowed tissue paper provided protection to whatever contents were underneath. Ellie hesitated. She felt as if she was intruding as she pictured Ben's father packing the box, ever so carefully.

Isn't it ironic? she thought. *When it comes down to it, it's the little things that matter the most.*

Getting through one layer and then another of the flimsy paper, Ellie put the box on the counter. The light was better there. Pulling back another sheet, Ellie felt her heart quicken. Lying there, side by side, were little snowmen. It was obvious they'd been hand-sewn. It was obvious they were very old. No two were alike. Some were taller. Some were shorter. None resembled the commercial ones mass produced somewhere and sold everywhere. The materials used might have come from old clothing, thought Ellie, like the woolen and flannel material her grandmother would de-button and de-zipper and cut into strips for braided rugs. Picking up one of the snowmen, Ellie could tell its face had been hand-painted. The detail was amazing. Curiosity got the best of her. Soon all the snowmen were on the counter. All had hand-painted faces. Some were little girls with rosy cheeks and long lashes. Some were moms. Some were dads with tall hats, and others were little boys with impish grins.

With the box empty and the contents sprawled out in front of her, it was apparent to Ellie that there was a story screaming to be told in the bits of fabric and artisan detail that had been wrapped up and stashed away. As she put the snowmen back and layered the tissue paper over them, her mind wandered. What were they saying to her? Why had Ben's father insisted on giving his son this particular box, above all the others he'd left behind?

Exhausted, Ellie put the box back up on the shelf and went to bed. Lying beside Ben who was still as much a turn-on as back in the days when she'd sit in the sun with her friends and pretend not to notice him, Ellie sensed that he'd need her more than ever before. With the wind sifting through the barren trees, the moonlight edged its way into their bedroom, which could have been a spread in some slick magazine.

Situated in the back of the house, the room was enhanced by antiques bought in and around Portsmouth on fall weekends, when getting away meant meandering through little shops while the smell of leaves and pumpkin lattes swirled about. Ben was the one who loved rummaging through those places in search of primitives. He'd turned the old carriage house sitting near the apple grove into a sort of workshop where he restored some of the stuff he'd found. That was his relaxation. Ellie found it ironic that he had the patience for such work.

"Craftsmen spent hours creating these pieces," he'd explain. "It's out of respect that I do what I can to preserve them."

As the wind circled about the old stone home, Ellie nudged closer to Ben. Her stirring woke him up for a second. Pulling her near, Ben fell back asleep. Ellie took comfort in his arms. The rest was left for another day.

Chapter Six

Early morning found Ben outside snow blowing. Despite whatever it was that he was dealing with, Ellie was glad to have him home. Now through the new year, he'd use his home office for any business. It had been a hectic year for his firm. Ellie realized that the perfectionist in him demanded the best from his associates. Stirring her coffee, Ellie concluded that perfectionism could be a hindrance when life throws its curves. That was why she worried. Ben lived by plans and exactness. Those snowmen in the box weren't planned. Ellie felt they could throw a mighty curve to a man already troubled. The first thing he asked when walking back inside was whether or not Andy was up.

"I haven't heard a thing, honey."

"Think I should wake him?"

Ellie didn't have the answer for that one. Movement from upstairs came just in time. To Ellie's surprise, Andy had decided to go with them. He didn't give a reason. Ellie didn't ask for one.

"Where's that old coat I'd wear skiing, Mom?"

"It's in the cellarway."

"Do you think you'll be warm enough?" asked Ben.

"I always used to be, Dad, when I was on the slopes."

Ben didn't push it. Instead he sat down with Andy for some breakfast. While they ate, Ellie packed a lunch.

"I was telling the guys how you saw Hendrix, Dad."

"Most of the performers up on that stage were relatively unknown."

"So cool you had a band."

"It was fun for a while. How's it working out with your playing in a band and school?"

"I don't want to go back."

"To school?"

"Right. I don't want to go back."

Snow trapped in little whirlwinds danced up and around the kitchen windows as Ben asked Andy to think about it before ruining his life. Ellie almost ruined the second batch of pancakes thinking of the consequences of Andy's decision. It didn't matter. Ben was back outside. Andy was getting his boots.

"Your father is right, Andy. You have to put serious thought into what you are considering. Earning a degree unlocks doors."

"Trouble is, Mom, I don't know what door I want to unlock."

"It will come to you."

"And if it doesn't?"

"You have to trust me when I say it will. It did for your father. It did for me."

"When you were my age, you didn't have many choices. Bet it was nursing or teaching."

"You may be right, but I enjoy what I do."

"I want to love what I do, Mom." With that, Andy went out the door.

Knowing that Henry was punctual like Ben and, just like Ben, expected everyone else to be the same, Ellie hurried, stopping to take something out for dinner. She was thankful she'd asked Ben to invite Henry to join them. The old man had a way with Ben, which seemed to have rubbed off on Andy. *Maybe he'll offer Andy some insight that only age can bring,* she thought. Ellie respected Andy for wanting to love whatever path he chose. She knew so many people unhappy in their career choices. Some felt trapped once children and a mortgage came along. They went one day to the next, waiting for retirement. Down deep, she thought Andy might have it right.

Chapter Seven

IT WAS A MARVELOUS DAY TO search for a Christmas tree. Standing on the back step, Ellie looked beyond the carriage house to fields dressed in sparkling white. Untouched, under the glimmer of the winter sun, it reminded her of a Currier and Ives painting. After all, there was a horse—actually two—and a grand, ornate sleigh, decorated in pine boughs and trimmed in strands of silver bells, waiting for them.

"Good morning, Henry," she said. "Thanks for taking us to the woods."

"It's my pleasure. I haven't hitched the team up for a good two weeks."

"I'm happy we're the reason."

"I wouldn't have missed this, Ellie. Getting the perfect tree is quite the task. Helen was particular. The tree had to be a balsam, and it had to fill the front parlor."

"Was that for you and Helen," asked Ben, "or for the kids who'd visit?"

"Oh, the tree was for those kids. There were so many over the years. So many kids who needed a place to call home, if only for a few hours."

"Things aren't always what they seem, even if you have a home," added Ben.

He didn't explain what he meant. It was quiet for a bit. Henry seemed to be able to read between the lines.

"That can be true about anything, Ben. It's how you handle it that makes the difference."

With that said, Henry gave the horses a final check. Then he boarded the sleigh and took the reins.

"I brought along some blankets," he told his passengers as they got situated. "You'll need them once we get going. It's always colder in the woods."

"Mind if I sit next to you?"

"I don't mind at all, Andy. Reminds me of when some of the older children—young teens, they were—asked to sit up here."

Henry turned around for one last look. He'd hitched an old wooden flatbed to the rear of the sleigh. They'd use it to carry the tree home. He also brought along two saws. From experience, he knew they'd need all the help they could get bringing down the tree.

"Helen would have loved this. It'd only be the two of us going. Once we got back, we'd have her soup and cornbread—warm up by the fire from the day."

As she listened to Henry, Ellie was struck by his silhouette against the crisp blue sky. With his billowing beard and black wool hat with earflaps and fur trim framing his wrinkled face, she realized what a strong character this gentle man had. His deep-set eyes reminded her of someone. She couldn't figure out whom. She forgot about it as Henry signaled to the horses. It was time to go find the Christmas tree in Santa's Christmas sleigh.

Chapter Eight

Once they traveled beyond stone walls and picket fences and over abandoned railroad tracks, it was all open fields to the backwoods. Henry owned the mighty parcel of land, along with other properties in the region. He'd been offered millions by developers but had no interest in selling any of it.

"Enough of nature has been turned into asphalt and condos," he'd tell those coming to him with those hefty offers. "I don't need the money, and even if I did, I wouldn't sell my soul to make it. Call me quirky, but for as long as I live, this land will remain untouched."

Despite being in the business of building, Ben agreed with Henry. He'd always choose rolling landscapes over slick construction jobs. He preferred going into abandoned places or deserted downtowns and restoring them. As with the primitives in the carriage house, aesthetics was a priority.

"How fast can they go?"

"After we get through this last thicket, you'll find out, Andy."

It didn't take long. With the clump of pines behind them, Henry signaled. The horses were off.

"Pull those blankets up, Ben!"

Henry's words drifted into the wind. It didn't matter. Ben had ridden with Henry before. Knowing what to expect, he put his arm around Ellie, pulling her closer. Even in the freezing cold, she felt his warmth, despite his distance. She tried not to let it ruin the moment, but that was nearly impossible when she remembered past Christmases when they'd choose a November weekend for shopping in the city. Ben would make reservations at the Plaza in early September. Ellie loved it there. A horse and carriage ride around Central Park was as much a part of their plans as was Ben surprising Ellie with a gift while riding into the night, covered in fancier blankets than the ones now covering them. Being the romantic that he was, Ben would point out that the gift wasn't a Christmas gift; rather, it was "a little something" to show her how much he loved her. Funny thing was, that little something was always Broadway tickets. Ellie loved Broadway. Just walking around Times Square brought her back to her senior year when she nailed the lead role in the school play. Everyone was amazed by her voice, even the young man who surprised her when returning home for opening night. Many encouraged Ellie to continue with her voice after graduation. She wasn't much of a gambler back then, plus her father insisted she go into nursing.

"You'll always have a job," he'd repeat whenever Ellie questioned his logic. He saw the world as black and white. That was how he ran his life and those of the people around him.

They didn't do the weekend in New York this year. Ben couldn't find the time. That letdown added to Maggie's email saying she wouldn't be home for Christmas. She'd decided to spend the holidays with associates. Skiing in the Alps was in her plans.

"It's a chance to network," she explained. "Anyone who's anyone will be there. I'll try to get back for a week in the summer."

Ellie had seen the disappointment in Ben's eyes. Maggie was Daddy's little girl. They'd spend a good part of a day out Christmas shopping, returning with their arms full of presents. So much was changing. Ellie felt as if she had no control over any of it. It wasn't about the gifts anymore. When she thought about that, it never was about the gifts.

The morning's brilliance was deceiving. While the temperature hovered around fifteen degrees, the wind chill factor made it even colder.

It didn't matter. With the horses galloping at full speed, Andy held on with all his might while Henry led his steeds through the powder-like snow. The once-distant tree line was suddenly in front of them. In an instant Henry pulled back on the reins. Into the woods they went.

The silence was deafening. Except for the horses snorting, any noise was cushioned by pine and balsam spread out as far as the eye could see.

"We'll take it slow. The best trees aren't too far in."

Henry was a master at leading the horses through and around the denseness. At one point he let Andy have a try.

"Hold the reins like so," he explained. "They'll do the rest."

Henry was right. While a few minutes before they'd been going full speed, the horses now gracefully lifted one hoof in front of the other. As they broke into the untouched snow, chunks of the stuff danced into the air.

"Snow's pretty heavy in here," said Henry. "It reminds me of winters long ago, before they started playing with the environment."

"You believe in that stuff, Henry?" Andy asked.

"Just saying. Winters used to be harsh, like winters should be. Otherwise you don't appreciate spring. You must be studying that stuff, aren't you?"

"Some."

"How do you study *some?*"

Wings fluttering up from a thicket startled the horses.

"Pull back, son. There's more grouse in those barbs."

A cloud of startled birds lifted up in front of them as Andy did what Henry directed. When the horses quieted down, deeper into the woods they went.

"So," Henry continued, "tell me how you study *some*. Seems to me studying is a part of college life. I realize you think you know it all, but believe me, you don't know a thing, even if you're hooked up to those contraptions."

"I get what you're saying, Henry, but I'm quitting school. I want to live life my way."

"You're quitting school to avoid earning a degree that will open doors for you?"

"There's no guarantee that it will."

"There's no guarantee on anything."

"I need some sort of a guarantee. That's why I started my band. I don't want to put off doing what I know I want to do—while I do what others think I should do."

Ellie and Ben were listening to the conversation. They'd known their son played in a band. They didn't know that it was actually his band.

Ben couldn't hold back. "I understand the freedom you are after, Andy. I respect you for that, but I don't want you to look back some twenty years from now with regret."

"If I don't go for it now, Dad, in twenty years I could look back and regret that I didn't listen to what makes me tick." Andy paused. "We've signed with an agent."

"But school," said Ellie. "You are still in school."

"Not much longer, Mom. I signed the contract before cutting a CD."

"What CD?"

"This one, Dad." Andy pulled a manila envelope from his coat pocket. "We're going on tour."

They didn't realize that they'd reached the pine grove, or that the sleigh had come to a halt, or that Henry was off the sleigh, releasing snowshoes strapped to the flatbed.

"I was going to give this to you and Mom for Christmas. I changed our name, Dad. Like it?"

While Henry pushed snowshoes into the snow, Ben unwrapped what was inside the mailer covered by newspaper and taped at both ends. Tears came to his eyes.

"The guys like the name as much as I do. You saw Hendrix. You saw the master on stage."

Maybe it was realizing this was a heartfelt conversation between a father and son, or maybe it was the way Ben looked at the CD. Either way, Ellie had seen him bite his lower lip like that before. She knew he was overwhelmed, but what she didn't know was the reason why.

"Dad? Don't you get it? I named the band after you."

"You shouldn't have, Andy. I don't deserve it."

"But Dad, you are *the Architect* in so many ways. I bet you could have soloed up on that stage."

Ben wrapped the CD back up and slid it inside the envelope. Handing it to Andy, he stood, jumped off the sleigh, and strapped on a pair of snowshoes. In seconds, he was going full speed through the drifts—running away to nowhere.

Chapter Nine

"Hey, Dad! Wait!"

Andy had never been on snowshoes, but that didn't slow him down. "Wait, Dad! I know I should have talked to you about quitting school, but it's my life, Dad!"

Ellie was out of the sleigh. She stood there, buried in snow. Watching Ben, she felt like she was watching a little boy lost and trying to find his way back home in the storm. In seconds her instinct proved to be true.

Ben kept up the marathon. It was Henry who waved the red flag. "Ben, stop! I know what's eating at you."

A breeze coming from behind them pushed some of the snow off branches as Henry called out again. "You can't escape it, Ben. You're not a quitter."

"Dad!" Andy was right behind his father now. "What's wrong? Dad! You're the best, Dad!"

Ben stopped as abruptly as he'd begun. Catching his breath, he lifted his face to the wind. With his eyes shut, he inhaled and then slowly exhaled, as if accepting the moment. With Andy by his side, they headed back to the sleigh. They didn't speak as snowbirds followed and rabbits skipping into the underbrush stopped. Mother Nature seemed to sense this man who embraced neglected objects was hurting.

Standing next to Ellie, Henry spoke in a whisper. "It's harder for a man to express his feelings, especially a proud man like your husband."

Henry doesn't know the Ben I do, she thought. *We have a connection.* Sometimes on warm summer evenings, when it was just the two of them in the stone home, they'd sleep on the screened-in sun porch on a pull-out sofa. It was nothing fancy. The feather mattress had its lumps. But it didn't stop the star-watching and the lovemaking, which took on even deeper meaning as years turned into milestones and worries came and went. Up until Ben's father died, they still couldn't get enough of each other. They'd still play classical music on their record console as pleasure turned to ecstasy.

But pleasure was far from her mind as Ben got closer. From the sadness in his eyes to the anger in his spirit, Ellie sensed that the Ben approaching was even more crippled than she'd realized. To her surprise, he grabbed hold of her. It wasn't out of love; rather, it was fear. Knowing him like she did, Ellie didn't wait for an explanation. He was holding on for dear life.

"Tell me, Ben," she said. "Whatever it is, we can get through it. That's what we've always done."

With tears streaming down his face, Ben whispered in her ear. His words were muffled. She didn't catch what he'd said. Pulling back, Ellie asked again, in a firmer voice, "Tell me, Ben. Tell me right now. Tell me what has taken you away from me."

Still clinging to her, Ben shouted, "I was adopted!"

Standing under branches resembling wings of angels laden in sparkling white, no one uttered a word. After having thought there was another woman, or that his firm was in trouble, or that he was ill, Ellie was caught off guard. Now she was the one who found it hard to speak.

"Did you hear me? I was adopted! I was adopted!" Ben shouted even louder. His echo came right back at him.

"But Ben—"

"I don't get it, Dad," Andy said, interrupting his mother. "You had parents. They were my grandparents. Grandpa took me fishing. Maggie and I would stay overnight. They took us to movies. They came for every birthday and Christmas."

"All I can say is that I'm not your 'best dad,' as you say I am, Andy. I don't know who I am. I was an orphan. My own mother didn't want me. I have no history—I don't know who came before me or who came before them. I couldn't say who I look like, or where my eye color comes from, or if I walk like someone or have quirks like any of my relatives, or if I have any relatives at all. I am a blank slate. I've lived a lie all my life. If I don't know who I am, how can I move on?"

Now that Ben had opened up, Ellie could take it from there. "I remember the weekend before your father passed away. You spent the night with him, and when you walked back though the kitchen door Sunday evening carrying that cardboard box, I sensed something had changed. Now I think I know what you talked about."

"I was sitting by his bed," said Ben. "He was rambling on about how he missed the woman I'd called my mother. He told me more than once how they'd met, and how it was love at first sight, and how they married despite their families telling them to wait. I asked him why they never had more children after me, and that's when he started to cry. I'd never seen him cry before. I sat there. I didn't know what to say. When he got himself together, he pulled me close, as if afraid someone else might hear—which I thought odd, as we were the only ones in the house. He hesitated, cried a little more, and then said, 'Your mother couldn't have children.'"

Ellie squeezed Ben's hand as he continued. For some reason, neither seemed bothered by the wind and snow.

"It didn't register, what he was telling me. At first I thought he meant she couldn't have any more children after giving birth to me, but then he told me to open the drawer in the stand next to his bed and hand him his leather binder. It held everything that had been a part of his life and, it turned out, mine as well. After fidgeting through layers of documents, he came to an envelope that was worn and wrinkled. I could tell it'd been opened several times. On the face of the envelope, in faded block letters, were the words ADOPTION PAPERS. He hesitated before handing it to me. He couldn't talk. He looked away as I read that everything I'd ever been told had been a lie, and that everyone I thought I knew I didn't. I sat there for the longest time, reading that paper over and over again."

"Did your father tell you anything more?"

"He explained how after his wife had miscarried, they were told she wouldn't be able to have children. He went on to say how the decision to adopt had been a tough one. They weren't sure if they'd be able to love another's child, but after they found me, their fears went away. He spoke of how they'd agreed not to tell me I was adopted. I think when he realized he was dying, he felt obligated to tell me the truth."

"So that means I have two sets of grandparents," said Andy.

"You'll never know one set. I'll never know who they were, or what they were like, or why they didn't want me."

"How can a mother not want her child?"

"For many reasons, Andy. I'll always wonder why my mother didn't want me."

"You weren't given any explanation as to who your birth parents were, Ben?"

"I asked, Ellie. I told him I needed to know since my life had suddenly become a jigsaw puzzle with the pieces all scattered."

"What was his response, Dad?"

"He said nothing. He seemed perturbed. He bolted out of bed and went to his closet. I kept up with the questions as he rummaged around but he ignored me. Instead he grabbed that box I brought home and climbed back in bed, exhausted. Once he could speak, he handed it to me, telling me my answers were inside. He explained that when I was brought to them on a cold winter night, the box came with me."

"Did you open it, Ben?"

"Once he fell asleep, I went downstairs. I put the box on the dining room table and sat there looking at it. I tried imagining who had put whatever it was inside, and who taped it up and made certain it was with me when I left wherever I was. I imagined all sorts of things were inside, like pictures and letters, but there were none included."

"So what was in it?" asked Andy, tightening the scarf around his neck.

"I'm certain he gave me the wrong box. He'd become so confused that last month. Most times he called me a dozen names before getting to Ben. I wonder if that name came with me, too. Anyway, all I found inside were a bunch of little snowmen. It was obvious they'd been handmade. Most of the materials used were worn and frazzled. I'm certain they were tree ornaments as they each came with a loop sewn to the top of their hats. I figured he'd made a mistake but I brought the box home anyway. I didn't want to hear it if I'd left it there."

"I would have gone searching in his closet, Dad. He was looking for something. Whatever it was it had to have been in there somewhere."

"I'd had enough. After he passed away, I thought I'd find what he was talking about, but I never did."

"Were those snowmen ever hung on any of your Christmas trees when you were growing up?" Ellie asked.

"I'd never seen them before. My adoptive mother was great for finding bargains, so I assumed she'd found them somewhere and stashed them away with all of her other buys."

"Funny how you automatically called the mother who raised you your *adoptive mother*."

"That's what she was, Ellie."

"I understand, honey. But she was the mother who'd been there for you. Your adopted parents did an outstanding job raising you. Your values, and the way you live your life and treat others, all come from their influence."

"For the most part I believe that to be true, but I think the core of who we are is born within us."

"Do you want to know who your birth parents were?"

"A part of me wants to know, Andy."

"I daresay that's the little boy in you," said Ellie.

"It is. The adult part tells me to leave it alone."

"I know you, Ben. You search for details. There are no other details more important than those of our very being."

"But what if I discover I wasn't wanted?"

"But Ben, what if you discover you were?"

Up to this point Henry had remained aloof, covering the horses in woolen blankets and scouting the edge of the pine trees. While not speaking, he stayed near enough to hear what was being said. With Ben questioning what he might discover should he pursue answers, Henry felt compelled to speak. "It's getting colder. We need to find the tree and head back."

Looking at Ben and then Ellie, he changed his tone. "This is not the place to get into what I am going to say."

Henry paused. Even the wind quieted as he continued. "Your birth mother loved you, Ben. It was hard for her to give you up. I will tell you all I know once we get back to your place."

"Just tell me my mother's name, Henry. I need to hear her name."

"Those of us who loved her called her Sophie."

It was Andy who found the tree. Amazingly they all agreed it was perfect.

"I love the bird's nest tucked back within the branches," exclaimed Ellie, who studied every tree that was ever brought into their home.

She wished Maggie could be with them more than ever as the mighty balsam was brought down. It took the three men to carry it to the flatbed and secure it in place.

The horses didn't need prodding. They knew the way.

Back in the kitchen, Ellie doctored her homemade soup and made a salad. She'd baked Ben's favorite bread earlier that morning so all she had to do was make her caramel sauce for the dessert and light the candles. The table was set. The wine glasses were out of the corner hutch. Ellie wanted every detail taken care of for the evening ahead, when details would be on the minds of all who'd gather around the oak table. Ellie found herself wondering how Henry fit into Sophie's story. As she stirred the soup and took one last look around, Ellie feared what lay ahead. *Why is it that at Christmastime, we expect our lives to be perfect when gathering with those closest to us?* she wondered. *Nothing is perfect—especially when it comes to family. And when that family proves not to be what we've been led to believe, anything can happen.*

Chapter Ten

After explaining to Henry that the vegetables in the soup, now dished up in ceramic bowls, were from her garden, Ellie added, "There is no recipe. Trick is in the seasonings and lots of *acini di pepe*."

"And bread—lots of good bread," added Ben, buttering his second slice.

"I don't remember you ever having a garden, Ellie."

"When the kids were little, there wasn't time, Henry, especially if I was working midnights."

"Why would you work midnights?"

"Because Andy, I did shift work. I had no choice."

"I wouldn't do it."

"You're going to find that when you're on the road, you'll have to do things you'd never before considered," explained Ben. "It comes with the package. It's called responsibility."

It was quiet for a few minutes as the light of the setting sun made its way through the stained-glass window Ben had surprised Ellie with one hot August afternoon. He loved surprising Ellie. There never had to be a reason.

Passing Andy the pepper, Ben got back to where they'd left off, asking Henry to tell him about Sophie.

As Ellie refilled the old man's bowl, Henry hesitated before answering. But once he started, he kept going, right up to dessert.

"Years back, there were orphanages. None of this *family care* stuff, where you wonder what the heck is going on. Anyway, kids ended up in orphanages for different reasons. In Sophie's case, she lost both her parents. They'd been out on the river harvesting ice. It was mid-February. The temperature was about twenty. Her mother stepped on a soft spot and went right through. Back then they were layered in fur and wool. The woman never had a chance but that didn't stop Sophie's father from going into the water after her. They both drowned."

Ben had so many questions.

"How old was she?"

"I'd say about fifteen … maybe sixteen."

"Was she from this area?"

"No. Sophie was French Canadian. I've never seen eyes so brown or skin so flawless. Her mother was American. Her father—I think his last name was Beauvais—was from somewhere in Quebec. "That's where she grew up, but after losing her parents, she was brought back to the States. Since no one took her in, she ended up with the nuns."

"The nuns?"

"They ran the orphanage. They depended on donations and the generosity of the locals. That's how she met David."

"David?"

"His mother cooked for the orphans at the summer camp. Let me explain. In the summertime, many of the orphans stayed at a camp not far from here. Except for Sophie, only the boys got to go. So getting back to David, he often accompanied his mother. Sometimes he'd sleep over in one of the tents."

"Tents?"

"Nine or ten tents were pitched in a half moon. That's where the orphans slept. There was a building for the nuns and a mess hall-type structure used for meals and indoor recreation. In the back was the kitchen and, behind that, two rooms converted into an area for Sophie."

"Why didn't she stay with the other girls at the orphanage?" Ellie asked.

"Most likely because she was the oldest girl. She helped in the kitchen. She looked after the little ones. The last summer I remember, she'd started her own garden. With David back home from overseas, he helped her keep it up. They spent a lot of time together."

Henry paused for more salad. He took his time, as if figuring what to say and what not to say.

"She'd blossomed into a real beauty by then. She must have been in her early twenties. She kept her long hair pulled back most of the summer, except for when she went swimming. Instead of wearing a cap, like girls did back then, she wore her hair down, making her look like a mermaid when she'd surface for air. She was a strong swimmer. Sometimes, on real humid evenings, she'd go down to the river to cool off. David would often accompany her. They ended up in the river. Those nearby could hear them in the water."

Looking at Ben, Henry remarked, "You have her hair, son. It was that dark brown with just a slight wave. She looked French Canadian, and I don't even know what I mean. Maybe it was her high cheekbones. She was stunning. Smart too. I think the nuns had their heart set on Sophie joining the convent. While she had the kindness of a nun, she had the looks and demeanor of a woman meant for a life on the outside."

"What brought you to that summer camp, Henry?" asked Ben.

"My father had been a farmer. There were seven of us kids, so there was nothing left over except for eggs. Because Dad suffered from asthma, when I got back from the war, I slowly took over the farm. None of the others wanted it. We'd do what we could to help the orphans. That meant bringing down eggs about every other day. I was the one who'd deliver them."

"When you say you'd bring the eggs down, where was this camp?" Again Ben needed the details.

"It was near the section of the Birch River that flows to the south of here, but you had to walk down through the woods to get there. The land was owned by a local family who donated it to the orphans every summer. A gravel road brought you in to where the pine and cedar surrounded the tents and buildings. That's as far as the road went. Most times I'd ride my horse in."

"Did you go down there a lot?"

"That one particular summer I did. Sophie fell in love with horseback riding. Sometimes she'd pack us a lunch if there were leftovers."

Clearing his throat, Henry continued. "We even rode in the winter. One time, that is. She'd been after me to go riding in the snow. I kept telling her how brutal January could be but she kept asking me. So one day I picked her up at the orphanage in my dad's truck and brought her to the farm. We saddled up and headed out. I don't think the nuns were pleased, but it didn't stop Sophie. The weather turned pretty quick. What started out as a sunny day was soon the worst blizzard in years. Luckily we found shelter in someone's closed-up cabin. Sophie never worried. She had a spirit about her. I've never known such a strong-willed woman. She had to be."

"Why do you say that?" Andy asked.

"She was orphaned. There's a difference between being an orphan and being orphaned. Some of those children never knew their parents. Sophie had memories. She knew them, and lost them, and grew up determined to make her way."

"What about those of us who learn as adults that we'd been given away? Where do we fit in?"

"You fit in the middle. You've grown up with a family who loved you. You remember nothing else, so you have to make a decision. Do you move on and keep your memories as they are, or do you go back to the beginning and search for answers?"

"I can't understand why this woman gave me up if she herself was orphaned."

"Sophie lived in a time when having a baby out of wedlock was a black mark against a woman for life. Women didn't have the options that are available today. They were conveniently sent away until the baby was born and then came back looking like they did when they left. Trouble with that is the damage is on the inside. A mother never gets over giving her baby away. She carries that child in her heart forever."

"Think my mother did?"

"Your mother was the most loving woman I've ever known."

Henry stopped, excusing himself, saying he had to check the horses. Ellie sensed there was a deeper story than the one being told. Eyes sometime say more than words. When he returned, he started in where he'd left off.

"I'm certain your mother kept you in her heart and mind every day of her life, Ben."

"She was an unwed mother?"

"Labeling people is something I don't do."

"I don't want you to think I was degrading Sophie. I was trying to figure things out. I need to know everything about my mother. I need to know my mother's story."

"I understand," said Henry. "It's your story too."

"Ben, would you mind if I clear the table and get the dessert out? It will just take a minute."

"That's fine, Ellie. How about helping me bring the tree in, Andy?"

"Too much talking can slow a man down." Henry was up and ready to assist.

"Who'd like coffee with their dessert?"

Even Andy said he'd like a cup.

"I left the tree stand out on the sun porch, Ben."

"Just like you always do."

"Just like I always do, honey."

"Traditions are important, aren't they?" Ben hesitated by the kitchen door. "What do I do with them?"

"Them?" asked Ellie.

"Traditions, Ellie. What do I do with them? How do I ignore what's been ingrained in me? Traditions are what we're about. I'm about nothing."

"You continue on, Ben. You and I, Maggie and Andy ... we have our traditions. The traditions you were raised with will remain a part of you but be open to new traditions. It's never too late for new traditions. They have to start somewhere at some point and most times they start without our even noticing."

"In other words, don't worry about what I don't know."

"That's how you and I chose to live, even before saying our vows under the trellis in my parents' backyard."

"You were stunning, Ellie. You took my breath away. I've missed you." Ben left it at that.

They brought the tree from the porch to inside the garage. That's as far as they got. The branches needed time to fall. As Henry continued with his story about a beautiful young woman and her child, Ben felt his heart opening. When that happens, nothing can stop it, especially at Christmastime.

Chapter Eleven

"Coffee's strong," said Henry, "just the way I like it."

"There's more, Henry."

"Thanks Ellie but one cup's fine. Strong and basic's the way to drink it. Have no use for those flavored coffees."

"Coffee's a big business these days," said Ben.

"Can't figure out why."

"It's all in the marketing. You can sell anything if the marketing's good."

"That's what my agent told me, Dad."

"I was going to ask you, Andy, before all of this came up. Did you have a lawyer look at your contract?"

"One of the guys has a brother who's a lawyer. He did all of that for us, Dad."

"I'll help you any way I can. I've made a few connections over the years."

"It's your support I'd like."

"You have my support, Andy. But as your parent, it gets back to responsibility. I feel I have a responsibility to ask the questions now instead of later."

"I understand. I appreciate your always being there for me."

"Your mother loved coffee." Henry abruptly took the conversation back to where he'd left off. "The nuns would make a little extra just for their Sophie when coffee was available to them."

"What a time that must have been," said Ellie. "I can't imagine how upset the nuns were with her."

"They were in the business of forgiving. When Sophie found herself in trouble, one nun in particular, who was quite young herself, made all the arrangements after the accident."

No one said a word while Henry took a bite of his rice pudding. Wiping the corners of his mouth with his napkin, he continued.

"David was thought to have been the love of Sophie's life. They spent a lot of time together. When David learned Sophie was expecting, he proposed. They were to be married in the spring, but fate had a different plan. Sorry to tell you this just matter-of-fact-like, Ben, but David was killed two weeks before the ceremony."

"So ... so David would have been my father? What happened?"

"An early thunderstorm came from nowhere when he was out mending fences. Lightning struck him. Sophie's the one who found him when he didn't show up at the orphanage for supper. The doctor said he died instantly."

"That's so tragic," said Ellie. "She lost her parents and then David."

"I told you she was a strong woman, Ellie. After losing David, she devoted her attention to the child she was bearing right up to when she went away."

"Where was I born?"

"The nuns kept Sophie pretty well secluded. I tried to see her several times but couldn't get through the front door. When she did leave, the story told was that she'd gone off to reflect on joining the convent. I never bought that. It didn't fit the Sophie I'd grown close to. Others thought it a little odd since she had plans to marry. They figured she was most likely consumed in grief. That one particular nun, whom I learned was Sr. Mary Beth, made arrangements for Sophie to go to their motherhouse ... somewhere in Pennsylvania, I think it was. It might have been Ohio. I can't remember. From there, she was placed in one of those homes."

"That's where I was born?"

"One cold October morning, that nun told me. I'd kept after her once Sophie was gone—kept bringing eggs to the orphanage. When she figured out that I asked about Sophie because I cared, she opened up. Labor had been long. They were worried that Sophie might not be able to deliver you, but she did—nine pounds, you were, and crying to boot."

"Did they have pictures of me? Are you certain I was that baby?"

"You are definitely Sophie's child. They wouldn't have allowed anything to happen to either one of you. Once Sophie was stronger, she returned to the orphanage. It was her home. She knew nothing else. But as the nun explained, "Sophie was devastated when having to leave her baby behind."

Henry stopped for a minute. No one said a word. They waited for more of Ben's story. "Not knowing what to do with her," he continued, "the decision was made to bring you back to the orphanage. It was made clear to Sophie that should an opportunity arise for you to be adopted, that adoption would take place. Only the nuns were to know that you were Sophie's child. No one was to give Sophie's child special treatment."

"Being a mother," said Ellie, "I can't imagine how hard it must have been for Sophie to treat Ben as if he was just another orphan."

"Surprisingly it was also hard for the nuns. By the time summer rolled around, you two were inseparable, Ben. The nuns redid the back of the kitchen area down at that camp to make room for you. To bring in extra money, Sophie took to sewing. She became a fine seamstress."

"Did you visit, Henry?" asked Ben. "Did you get to see Sophie again? Did you see me as a child?"

"Fate can sometimes put us on paths other than the ones in our hearts. While Sophie was away, my father died. I was left with all of it, including an ailing mother. That's when I met Helen. She was a fine woman from a good farming family just over the county line. We married in the spring—a few months after you came back. I made a decision not to bother Sophie. Some things are best left as they are. I'd see her on occasion when I was asked by the nuns to help them out. When the orphanage was closed, I kept track of her for as long as I could."

"Why didn't you ever tell me any of this, Henry? We've worked side by side for years. We've spent hours talking. How could you keep this from me?"

"It wasn't my place, Ben. I kept track of you on the sidelines. I told myself back when we did our first project together that should the time come when I felt I should speak up, I would. That time is now. Sr. Mary Beth told me Sophie was never the same after your adoption, but she had no other choice. That's what she agreed to when they brought you back to be with her."

"She could have moved away somewhere with me. She could have disappeared into a big city and no one would have cared."

"It wasn't that easy. Besides having to deal with the nuns, when you were a little over six years old, your mother was stricken with polio. On top of that, orphanages everywhere were closing. When your adoptive parents came looking for a child and decided on you, the papers were hurried along before the place shut down. Sophie was sent off to a hospital and, from what I understand, was kept there for quite some time. She ended up with a bum leg. Luckily, she could still use her hands for sewing."

"Why didn't you adopt me, Henry? You and Helen never had children. If you cared so about my mother, why didn't you step in?"

Andy's cell phone interrupted the moment. He didn't bother to answer. He turned the phone off. "Sorry about that, Dad."

"It doesn't matter, Andy. It's a little late for the what-ifs."

"Helen suffered a miscarriage, Ben. It happened in the heat of haying season. She'd decided to bring us fresh water out in the back fields. To get there, she had to cross over an old plank bridge. Helen was eight months along, and with those planks being so uneven, she lost her balance. She twisted her ankle and fell. The doctor told us the baby was a good size but the cord wrapped around his neck. He was perfect, Ben. Turned out, though, God had other plans."

"Excuse my ignorance, Henry. I didn't mean to attack you. You've always been there for me. I am so sorry for your loss. I never knew."

"Older you get, the more you realize most everyone has secrets kept locked up tight. It's the only way sometimes. For a long while we blamed each other, especially when Helen was told she wouldn't be able to carry another baby to full term. We lived in near silence. We couldn't grasp hold of our sorrow. But that changed one night in early December with a knock at the front door. It was one of the nuns from the orphanage. She'd come to ask a favor." Henry stopped to ask Ellie for a glass of water. "I haven't talked so much in years."

Clearing his throat, Henry continued. "Helen invited her in. It was one of those blustery nights when you think most would be staying home curled up in blankets, and here was this nun with only a cloak wrapped around her shoulders. Helen led her into the front parlor where I was sitting. That was the first night since losing the baby that Helen and I sat and talked longer than a few minutes. Granted, there was a nun between us, but that was the beginning of our accepting our loss—thanks to you, Ben."

"Me?"

"Yes you, Ben. The nun was there to ask if I'd do them a favor. Now, when a nun asks such a thing, you know who is asking so I sat up and listened.

"Getting to the point, she explained that the orphanage would be closing its doors the end of that month. 'The order's come down from the motherhouse,' she said. 'With the state ready to initiate foster care, we need to shut down immediately. It's a sad day,' she continued. 'The convent is being sold. We're being sent elsewhere. All the children need to be ready to go before Christmas.'

"Both Helen and I asked how we could help. Suddenly we weren't blaming. We were giving. The nun explained, 'We've finalized our last three adoptions.' That's when Sister Mary Beth brought your name into the conversation. She thought it'd be fitting if those three children were delivered to their new homes on Christmas Eve. That nun told me that Sister Mary Beth felt it'd be ideal if I delivered the children by horse and sleigh. When Helen left the room for a minute, the nun told me one of the children was Sophie's boy. I broke down. I plain reacted. I thought of those horseback rides... thought about the baby I'd lost. I was embarrassed for the tears. The nun told me tears are God's way of healing. Later on, when it was only Helen and I, we talked about our loss, and

Sophie—to a point, that is. Now, looking back, I realize Helen never accompanied me to the orphanage when I was asked to help out. She stayed away."

The sound of the wind chimes hanging from the maple by the back porch made it clear that the weather was turning. Ben asked if there was more coffee.

"I'll make a fresh pot, honey," said Ellie.

"If you don't mind," said Henry, "I'll check the horses again."

"Put them in the barn."

"I already did, Ben." Standing by the back window, Henry added, "That Christmas Eve was a spectacular night. I've never seen such a sight. The stars and the moon were shining their brightest, guiding us along."

"Was it hard letting me go?"

"I never let you go, Ben."

"Who was with us in the sleigh?"

"It ended up you and me."

"Tell me about that night, Henry. Tell me about the night I was no longer Sophie's boy."

Chapter Twelve

Ellie carried the serving tray, with dessert dishes refilled and more coffee, into the front room where Ben had the fire roaring. Once Henry was back inside, the four gathered around the fireplace to hear of that Christmas Eve long ago.

"It took me a good two, two-and-a-half weeks to ready the sleigh. Helen told me it looked fine, but I'd become obsessed with trying to make everything perfect. I know it was because of Sophie. I couldn't stop thinking about her lying in some strange hospital, sick more about her little boy than the polio that had crippled her. That's why the reins were cleaned to the point of being silky to the touch. I freshened up the runners with paint. Helen darned several holes in the seats. Then I got my saddle soap out and scrubbed them clean. I even obsessed over the horses. 'Think the dappled one is a good choice?' I'd ask Helen about every evening at supper.

"One evening she told me not to ask her again. She told me she was tired of living in Sophie's shadow. That was our final discussion about that Christmas Eve. Helen stayed home when it finally came. Sister Mary Beth accompanied me on the first two stops. When it came to you, Ben, she asked me to take her back to the orphanage. She excused herself, saying, 'I pray God understands, but my heart is too heavy. I know Sophie's boy is in good hands with you, Henry. May God bless you and keep you, my little one.'

"Those were Sister Mary Beth's last words to you. She jumped down off the sleigh and never looked back. I could hear her sobbing as she ran up the steps. You, being so young, Ben—you didn't understand. Wrapped up from head to toe, with your face framed by one of those knitted toques, you resembled the teddy bear you were hugging. Sister Mary Beth told me it'd been the last thing your mother made you."

"Was I afraid?"

"No not at all. You knew it was Christmas Eve. You'd been told you were getting a home with a mommy and daddy and even a Christmas tree. You'd never known Sophie as your mother. She was Sophie to you, so it wasn't as if you felt you were being taken away. It was just the opposite. You were excited. Top that with riding in a decorated sleigh being pulled by a team of galloping horses, and you were bubbling over with joy; pointing to one place and then the next, wondering which one was yours. Pulling up in front of that clapboard house with its small front porch, I saw magic in your eyes. And when your mommy and daddy rushed out the door that was decorated in balsam and pine, you jumped up and held out your arms. You knew you were home."

"Did you say good-bye to me right there?"

"I followed the three of you inside where I handed your father your bag and a cardboard box. The first thing you noticed was the tree and the presents underneath it. Then your attention went to the stocking hanging by the fireplace. The last I saw you, you were in your mother's arms as she carried you upstairs to see your bedroom. Reaching the top of the stairs, you turned and waved good-bye to me. I thought of Sophie all the way back home."

"Would anyone like a glass of wine?" Ellie kept talking as she filled the tray with empty cups and dishes. "I think we need to wind down. It's been an emotional day."

"No, thank you," said Henry. "I should be on my way."

"Do you think Sophie's still alive, Henry?" Ben couldn't let the day go.

"I've wondered that over the years. Once the convent closed, I lost track of Sister Mary Beth. Time has a way of tucking such matters away in a place that's best left alone. That's what I've tried doing with Sophie."

"But she's my mother." After a pause, Ben asked Henry if the summer camp was still around.

"It is, although it remains unused. I'm sort of the unofficial caretaker of the property."

"Is it far?"

"Why?"

"I'd like to go there."

"Maybe in the spring we could get in. It'd be near impossible before then."

"I'd like to go as soon as possible."

"Did you hear what I said, Ben?"

"I heard a man afraid of going back to a place that is painful for him. I understand that, but I need to go back to move forward."

"I'll take that glass of wine, Ellie." Henry sat back down. He knew that once Ben had a thought, nine times out of ten he'd follow through despite obstacles that would stop most people. "Sleigh is the only way to get down in there this time of the year. The snow has to be even deeper than where we were today."

"So we go in prepared. Approximately how far do you think it is?"

"That depends on the weather. That will determine which way we take in."

"When can we go?"

"We'll have to watch the forecast."

"When it looks like a go, I want to go, Henry."

"I don't follow those weather map people. I prefer the moon."

"The moon?" asked Andy.

"Yup. My father used the moon to predict the weather. He'd often say if there's a ring around the moon, then snow is on the way. Surprisingly with all the crazy stuff going on with the environment, that old adage still holds true. But you decide, Ben. I'll be ready whenever you make the call."

"I'm not sure this is such a good idea, Ben."

"Why, Ellie?"

"Why go back there? It won't change a thing. What do you expect to find? It's been abandoned for years. No one is there."

"If there's a possibility Sophie is alive, I want to know. Maybe there'll be some sort of clue. I don't know what I'm after, but I have no other choice than to make the attempt, Ellie."

"I understand, honey. I know you. What worries me is that what you discover might not be what you are seeking."

"Then at least the blanks will be filled in. You said earlier there are no other details more important than those of our very being. You were right, Ellie. I have to go."

Ben had a way of getting to the core of things. He did it every day. Ellie made no reply except to remind him that Christmas was eight days away.

"Knowing you as I do, Ben, I'm sure you'd like to make the hike before Christmas."

"You know me well, Henry."

"Count me in, Dad," said Andy.

Henry volunteered to help put the tree up in the morning. With that decided, they said good night. Exhaustion had taken over as embers burned and hearts ached for a woman who once swam like a mermaid on hot summer nights, when life was innocent and full of promise. While snowflakes fell, thoughts of a Christmas Eve of long ago lulled the little boy inside the grown man to sleep. We never lose the child within us. It's always there, if we have the faith to embrace the innocence and sometimes the pain.

Chapter Thirteen

Early the next day Ellie called the hospital. Her seniority made it possible for her to take more days off than scheduled. With a fast-moving snowstorm behind them, Ben made the decision to go in. Ellie explained that the timing was good. She had Christmas under control.

"Since Maggie's in Europe and Andy's asking for nothing but money, there isn't the rush this year. The cookies are baked for the auxiliary. I sent Abbey's family their box earlier in the month."

Ellie and her cousin Abbey had been close growing up. They were always together. One of Abbey's sons was filming a documentary in North Africa. He'd emailed Maggie thinking they might possibly connect over the holidays.

"Family is a funny thing, isn't it?" Ellie said to Ben as they finished rearranging the front room for the tree. "No matter how many friends we have, it's family we look for at Christmas."

"I wonder if I'll find a new family," said Ben.

"It wouldn't be a new one, honey. It'd be an extended one."

"If Sophie... if my mother is alive, do you think she's thought about me, Ellie?"

"I'm certain she's never stopped thinking about you. When you give birth, you play that moment over and over in your mind. That child forever remains your baby."

"I still remember how sweltering it was in that hospital room when you were in labor for Maggie. I felt so useless."

"When I was certain I couldn't go on, you stayed by my side and told me I could, Ben. That final push, when I was beyond exhaustion—you were the strength that got me though. To think of the courage Sophie had, to endure labor alone and then to let you go for a better life is daunting. You have her determination, Ben."

"I wonder what else? I wonder about David and his family. So many questions that need answers and I don't even know if she's alive. That's why I have to go back there."

"You're a man who fits things together. I would expect nothing less of you than to try to gather pieces of your life."

"I didn't mean to shut you out, Ellie. I felt as if I'd lost my identity. I felt I'd lose you, too."

"Remember that time we went hiking and got lost?" she asked. "We fought the rain and the wind. The lightning was terrifying, yet you never doubted. You kept me calm. You told me we'd make it out of the woods. Now I'm telling you we will make it out of the woods again."

Pulling Ellie close, Ben unbuttoned her sweater—to a point. Following the outline of her lips with his fingertips, Ben slowly brought her to him and kissed her in a way he hadn't kissed her since being handed his adoption papers. Ellie responded. She'd missed him. If it weren't for Andy being upstairs, the two might have gone to their pullout sofa on the screened-in porch with storm windows now in place. But they knew they had to stop. It wasn't easy. Ben pulled her closer. Moving her sweater off her shoulders, he kissed her neck over and over.

"Oh, how I've missed you, Ellie."

"I've laid beside you, aching for you, Ben."

A cell phone ringing brought the two back to the reality of the day. It was Henry. Like Ben, he knew this was the time to go.

"I don't have to check those weather people to know this system's going to be here a while. I say we go first thing tomorrow. I'll be over later to help you with the tree."

Ben agreed. The plan began to take shape.

After Andy got up and showered, he grabbed a quick breakfast and headed to the door. "I'll be back by supper time," he said, pulling a hoodie over his head with one hand, holding onto his guitar with the other.

"Henry will be here in the morning, Andy."

"I'm with you, Dad."

"Your mother and I want to sit down with you and talk about your band and your tour, and where school might fit in at some point."

"We'll talk, Dad. Later."

The stone home was quiet. Except for an occasional cluster of little birds at the feeders, the winter day was as peaceful as it was beautiful. Since Henry wouldn't be coming to help with the tree until mid-afternoon, Ben took Ellie's hand and led her onto the sun porch. Words aren't needed when passion takes flight and classical music mingles with the scent of pine and cinnamon. There's something about snow and winter—if you listen.

Chapter Fourteen

Henry had been earlier than usual the day before, making Ellie and Ben scramble off the sun porch and get the tree up. So this morning, Ben cleared away what little snow fell overnight and made sure Andy was up and showered while Ellie made breakfast. When Henry knocked at the back door, Ellie had a cup of coffee ready for him.

"I added your touch of sugar."

"Thank you, Ellie." Taking a sip, Henry sat down at the table. "Sure is a clear day out there."

Pouring a half-cup, Ben explained there was a cold front moving in about midnight.

It didn't matter to Henry. "Sooner we get going, the sooner we'll be out of there and back home."

Ben knew what that meant. Henry was eager to leave. They were packed up and in the ornate sleigh in less than twenty minutes. With Andy by his side and Ellie and Ben wrapped in blankets, Henry picked up the reins. After doing a double check, they were off.

"Are we headed the same way where we got the tree, Henry?"

"For a while we are. Then we're on our own."

With his head down, Andy whispered. "I wanted to ask the other day; this is the sleigh, isn't it?"

"I wondered if you'd remember, son."

"When you're a kid and someone tells you they have a sleigh that brings kids to families, you don't forget. You might not understand what that means, but you don't forget. So this is that sleigh—the sleigh that brought my dad to his family?"

Henry nodded. Andy understood. Words weren't needed. In fact, no one spoke as the horses forged ahead. Snow spraying up from their hoofs sparkled in the winter sunlight. Soon the line of tall pines framing the woods was in view. But instead of going straight toward the trees, Henry led the horses another way. Even though the snow was deeper, the horses kept going. With their manes in flight, they seemed to be soaring past thickets and brambles, around fences and over creeks, until Henry pulled on the reins in front of a wooded area that appeared as if it had been left alone for years. Squirrels scurried under branches. Rabbits hurried away.

"I didn't think I'd remember. I haven't seen it in winter for quite some time."

Jumping off the sleigh, Henry asked Andy to get the snowshoes he'd strapped to the back while he tended to the horses.

"So we're going in on snowshoes, Henry?"

"I'm sure the horses could get us down there, Ellie, but I'd rather play it safe. It'll be an easy trek. Next time we'll take the sleigh in!"

It wasn't until Henry and Andy started into the woods that Ben reacted to the surroundings.

"Okay, honey?" Ellie asked.

"I've been focused on finding clues while never considering I'd be walking in my birth mother's footsteps."

"And yours as a little boy. A part of you never left this place."

It looked like it was snowing but it was the wind filtering through the branches as a little boy now grown stepped back in order to move ahead—but to where?

Chapter Fifteen

BEN LED ELLIE ALONG A TRAIL freshly etched by snowshoes. The farther they went, the statelier the pines seemed to be standing. Birch and cedar filled in the gaps. The forest appeared untouched. No loggers had made inroads. No vandals had destroyed what wasn't theirs. And NO HUNTING signs were absent. There didn't seem to be a need for them. There were no toppled pines dragged away for Christmas trees. There were no tracks made by snowmobiles.

"I kind of like snowshoeing," said Ellie. "Maybe I'll get cross-country skis."

"Maggie would be surprised, honey!"

"So would I, Ben!"

Rounding a curve marked by a mighty elm, Ben spotted the two ahead of them. "There's a sight. A young man is following an old man on a quest to find answers. Maybe that old man will offer more of his wisdom to the conversation. I don't want to see Andy make a mistake."

"How so?"

"We know how important a degree is, Ellie. It opens doors that otherwise would be out of reach. It gives one a foundation to build on. He'll want to get married, raise a family. How can he build a future running around in a band? I did that. It's a fantasy when you're that age. You're defined by your guitar."

"You never took your skill to the next level."

"Playing the guitar back then was like your wearing flowers in your hair. We all tried desperately to look the part, especially with the unrest and change in the air. But it didn't mean we actually lived the part."

"I can't believe I'm the one backing Andy's decision and you are on the sidelines, playing it safe. My first reaction was that he couldn't quit school. What would happen if he didn't graduate with that rolled-up piece of paper in hand? But I've thought it over, and you should too, Ben. You've done it your way since I met you, and now your son wants to do the same."

"But remember, Ellie, I went to school for years."

"True—and also true is the fact that you went against your father who told you there's no money in building things. He wanted you to take over his business."

Stopping to adjust one of his boots, Ben asked why she was supporting a decision that he felt could ruin Andy's life.

"I went from high school to nursing school," Ellie explained. "I played it safe. I listened to limited advice given by a school counselor who had no use for girls interested in anything other than the norm. It was my father who took me for the interview. It was my father who insisted I go into nursing. I never said anything about what I might want to do with my life. My dream of making it with my voice back when kids my age had number-one hits on *Bandstand* disappeared. Most likely nothing would have come from my singing, but I'll never know. I never followed my passion, Ben. There are times when I'm reminded of that and when that happens, way down deep inside I wonder if only for a moment. I'm aware of the risk Andy is taking. I don't know what the future holds for him. But look at us. We are trudging through the woods searching for answers to questions we never knew existed a year ago. No one knows what's in the future. But I do know that if nothing comes of Andy's music, at least he won't wake up someday, retired from some job, and wondering, '*What if?*'"

Looking down the path Ben could see Andy waving at them to hurry up. He remembered when he was Andy's age and out to claim the world just as Hendrix and Dylan had done. While he loved what he was doing and felt great satisfaction in the creative process he'd chosen, Ben connected with his son's passion felt when fingers touch taut strings and music is created. He'd never wondered, '*What if?*' But maybe Andy would. It would be a gamble, but so was searching for a woman who had ridden horseback on the gravel road now buried in snow.

"I get it, Ellie. I do support Andy. While I want our children to be secure, I also want them to feel fulfilled. Risk-taking builds character, and that's something not learned in a classroom."

"He gets that from you, Ben."

"Hopefully we'll discover where I got it."

Faint outlines of buildings could be seen ahead. Andy and Henry waited for Ellie and Ben; then together they proceeded into a summer camp that was dressed in winter.

Chapter Sixteen

Henry took the lead. Except for the shuffling of snowshoes, and a slight wind rustling pines heavy with snow and brown leaves still hanging on branches of poplar and maple trees, it was quiet as they made their way around a partial stone wall and into an open area void of any trees.

"This is where the tents circled around," Henry told them. "They were made of heavy canvas. When the sun hit them in the morning, they were like saunas. As soon as the boys woke up, they'd run outside and wait in line for one of the nuns to bring them down to the river for a swim. Over there, under that big oak, was where the nuns sat when it was too hot to do much else. They'd sit in those old enamel-type chairs with a small table in front of them and sip on lemonade and fan themselves with whatever they could find. Even with the snow, it looks the same. It feels as if they'll be back when summer comes again."

"I don't see any signs of life," said Ellie. "No tracks in the snow. I can't believe it's been left alone."

"There's a spirit here," explained Henry. "There's a sense of history to this place that warrants respect."

"Where was Sophie's garden?" Andy asked.

"Back in the field, behind where the nuns sat. If she was out there, I could see her when I rounded the corner by the big elm. She knew what time of day I'd be coming. She'd take off her straw hat and start waving the minute she…"

Henry abruptly changed the subject. He pointed to a building. "The building where the nuns slept looks smaller. Guess that's what happens when you reach my age. Hard to believe four and sometimes five slept in there."

"Can we go inside?" Andy was at the steps, pushing away snowdrifts.

"I can't see why not. Try the door."

Andy gave a shove. The door opened without a problem. Henry had no interest in going inside. He told the others he'd meet them in the big building.

"I see what Henry meant by the place being small," said Ellie.

"Maybe they had bunk beds, Mom."

"Look. Over here." Holding onto a clipboard, Ben was rummaging through lined paper, yellow with age.

"What is it, honey?"

"Looks like a schedule. First names are listed with times after each. Appears they had chores and they rotated weekly. I don't see Sophie anywhere."

"I bet she stayed in the kitchen, Ben."

"Can you believe it, Ellie? I was here running around and playing while my mother worked. I wish I could remember."

"The mind is a funny thing. Give it time."

The other building had been painted forest green but the years hadn't been kind. Some of the boards were rotting. A few of the windows were missing glass while others were cracked. A screen door, with some of the screen pulled away from the molding, was followed by a door with a plaque saying DELIVERIES AROUND BACK. Andy led the way inside to a large area with a cement floor and rows of tables with benches. A light layer of frost coated the wooden beams. It even created intricate designs on the windows.

"Breathtaking!" Ellie was amazed by what she saw. "It looks like an ice castle."

"This is where the orphans ate," explained Henry. "After their meals, the tables were used for games, or art projects, or doing schoolwork.

Some of the boys needed tutoring. The nuns did that. When Sophie was older, she was tutor, chef, and gardener. On rainy days the tables were piled on top of each other, over in that corner, and the place turned into a basketball court. They had Ping-Pong tables too. Some Friday nights, one of the priests would bring down a projector and they'd watch slides against the wall. They'd have popcorn when it was available."

"Why did they leave it like this?" Ben questioned.

"It had to do with funding. They tried to rent the place out to organizations during the summer months but that never got off the ground. Eventually all their equipment was out-of-date and the building needed repair. They must have decided it was cheaper to leave it as is."

Walking through a doorway without a door into the kitchen, they quieted down. It wasn't until they'd been inside a few minutes that Henry spoke.

"When Sophie first came, David's mother was doing the cooking. As Sophie grew older, she developed a knack in the kitchen. Once Sophie reached a certain age, they let David's mother go and put Sophie in charge of meals. It looked good in the budget. It kept the board happy. Sophie was fine with the setup. And when you came along, those renovations were made to the back area to give you and your mother space."

"How did that get by the board?" asked Ben.

"It happened just as the state deemed that certain changes had to be made to the kitchen or they'd close the place down. The approved plans didn't include the detail that the pantry indicated was actually your room or the extra prep room your mother's."

"How'd it pass inspection?" Ben wondered.

"Lots of prayers," chuckled Henry.

"Look at those ovens," remarked Ellie.

"The boys had good appetites. With that French Canadian in her, Sophie developed a flair for baking. Everyone looked forward to Sunday night dinner. Even some of the priests would come to enjoy the meal, especially the dessert."

"She had lots of storage area," Ellie noted.

"Sophie needed it. The number of orphans increased every summer."

"She made tarts!"

Ben was standing by one particular oven, pulling on the handle. He did this a few times, pulling it open and then closing it, as if studying its every movement; but it wasn't the movement that had Ben's attention.

"I remember that creaking," he said. "I'd be lying in bed early in the morning, and most every morning I'd hear bowls clanging, and a mixer whipping, and the oven door creaking, over and over. It was such a shrill creaking that I covered my ears with my pillow."

Moving further into the room, Ben blurted out, "Jam tarts! I can smell them baking. They were made from leftover pie-crust dough."

Ben looked around. "Over there. That's where there used to be an old cupboard sort of thing. Like that Hoosier cabinet we bought outside of Portsmouth. Know which one I'm talking about, Ellie? I have it in the barn. I've been meaning to strip it down and put it in the kitchen. It has the flour bin and the bread drawer with the metal lid and the slide-out shelf. That's what sat here. There was a cabinet right here like the one I bought. My mother would pat the dough into a ball. Then she'd hand me a rolling pin so big I could hardly hold onto it. But I did. I'd roll the dough out on the cabinet shelf. Then we used a cookie cutter to cut out fancy shapes. My mother did the rest. After she filled each tart with jam she'd made from wild strawberries, she put them in the oven on one large cookie sheet. I can smell the cinnamon and the nutmeg and the sweet dough. They were piping hot when they came out of this oven with its creaky door. The jam would be oozing out of the corners of the tarts. I always got to have one still warm with a glass of milk."

Ben stopped. He struggled to get his next sentence out.

"I remember her. I remember standing next to her while she spooned the jam onto the dough. Her hair was just as you described, Henry. Her eyes were soft, loving. She called me her little helper. She picked me up and called me her little helper. She smelled like Ivory soap."

Ben knew where he was. From the kitchen, he went farther back, past what he remembered to be his mother's room, into a barren room once painted sky blue but now dingy with broken shades. There was still a bed with a twin mattress, blankets, and a pillow without a pillowcase against a far wall. A small desk with a matching stool sat under the only window. The closet door was open wide enough that boxes could be seen stacked up until they hit a few wire hangers with nothing on them. Lining the wall were sheets of paper covered with crayon scribbles kept in place by straight pins. Some had fallen to the floor. Some were curled up into knots.

By the time the others caught up with Ben, he was standing by the desk. Henry stayed in the doorway while Ellie and Andy went inside.

"I vaguely remember being in here, playing, and hearing the music from my mother's radio in the kitchen. Bits of things are coming back to me."

Opening the single drawer, Ben found scribbles like those on the wall. There were broken pencils, and parts of crayons, and a few box tops from Cracker Jack boxes, and even some plastic surprises from inside those boxes. Pulling the drawer out farther, he found pennies and ticket stubs. But it was an envelope with beautiful penmanship that made his heart quicken. Ben picked up the envelope. Sitting on the edge of the bed, it took him several minutes to simply say, "My mother called me Benny. Look. See. She wrote it on this envelope. *To my Benny. Love forever, Mommy.*"

Ellie sat next to him. She didn't say a word as Ben studied the envelope, rubbing his fingers over words written so long ago. Ever so carefully, Ben opened the envelope and pulled out a card. It was a Christmas card with a smiling snowman hugging a little boy. But it was the inside that mattered. In her own words, Sophie told her little boy how much she loved him and how she'd never forget him.

> *To my Benny,*
>
> *I wish you a Merry Christmas, this year and every year. My gift to you is wrapped in love and kisses and not given without great thought and many prayers. Every child deserves a family—especially my Benny. I will love you forever and think of you every moment of every single day. You will always be in my heart, my sweet child. I wish you happiness and sunshine and dances around the kitchen, like those we shared.*
>
> *My love forever and ever, beyond the rainbows outside your bedroom window, my Benny.*
>
> *Love forever,*
> *Mommy*

No one could speak. A few minutes later, Henry broke the silence.

"Sophie never gave you up, Ben. She gave you a better life." Henry felt he had to point out the difference, for Sophie's sake.

"She must have written the letter after the adoption was finalized, honey."

"Why do you think she put the letter here in my old desk drawer, Ellie?"

"I can only guess. I'd say she decided to put the letter in a place where you spent time together. It must have felt safe. Writing it was probably something she had to do, to make sense of giving you up. It wasn't meant to be mailed."

"Think I should leave the card?"

"That's up to you."

Ben put the card back in the envelope. After hesitating, he put the envelope in his coat pocket. "It's all I have of her. I don't want to lose it."

"Dad. Come here!"

Andy was in the closet. "Look what I found behind these boxes." He opened his fist. "It's a chimney from a Lincoln Logs set, Dad.

"There have to be more."

Andy pushed more boxes aside but found nothing.

"Let's open the boxes," suggested Ben.

Andy did as his father directed.

"Only clothes in this one, Dad. They're all baby clothes."

Ben opened another and found birthday cards and more drawings. In another he found a few stuffed animals and baby blankets. He didn't stop. Tearing open another, Ben's face told the story. There it was. There was the toy canister he'd have flashbacks about. It was right there in front of him, beside a worn, brown teddy bear with a black button nose that looked like it had been sewn on more than a few times.

Over the years he'd caught glimpses of himself as a little boy, building homes and cabins and tall buildings, all with green roofs and some topped with red chimneys. He'd told his children about playing with the logs and sketching his ideas on a white pad of paper with lines, but he didn't know where until now. He'd been sitting at that small desk just a few feet away. He was certain. While his mother cooked, Ben had played with his Lincoln Logs. Sophie would check on him. He remembered her going on and on about whatever it was that he was constructing. She'd tell him every time that he was going to be a great builder.

"This is where all that happened. I'd leave what I'd built until the next time. Then I'd bulldoze it with my hands and start all over."

Ellie rummaged through a few of the boxes. "These clothes must have been everything you ever wore. There are baby nightgowns to toddler's shorts and shirts in here." Something else caught Ellie's attention. "Mind if I open this box, honey?"

It was a square one with a frayed ribbon.

Ellie could tell by Ben's expression that he was saying, *Go ahead.* Slipping the ribbon down, Ellie took a corner of the box and pulled. The sight of little ducks and bunnies running after a little boy with a kite told Ellie that this was Ben's baby book. It was in fairly good shape. She handed it to Ben.

Besides pressed flowers and leaves, Ben discovered details of his birth. They weren't entered in the baby book. They were written on pages of stationary clipped together and tucked inside. When Ben opened the book, the pages caught Ben's attention. At first he didn't realize what he'd found. After scanning a few paragraphs, he felt the need to share what Sophie had shared. His voice was shaky as he explained that Sophie hadn't been alone.

Sister Mary Beth was with her. "On a blustery Sunday in October, when my water broke at 2:32 in the morning," Ben read aloud, "I packed up my belongings and went up to the delivery floor. While I waited to be examined, I stood in front of the window of the nursery. So many babies—there were so many babies. I wondered where they would go. I wondered what will happen to my baby."

Ben took a deep breath before adding a comment.

"She goes on to tell about finally getting into a hospital gown as Sister Mary Beth is called. She includes a side note explaining that Sister Mary Beth had arrived earlier in the week."

He stopped, but only for a moment. "Labor was long and gruesome. Forceps were used to pull my baby away from me. My perfect baby boy was born at 11:16 that morning. They must have been in a hurry to get me out of the way. There were three other girls in labor. Sister Mary Beth never left my side. It was Sister Mary Beth who allowed me five minutes to hold my baby."

"She explains how that was an exception. The rule stood that all newborns were to go directly to the nursery. She credited Sister Mary Beth for breaking the rule, if only for a few minutes. 'I stayed there for ten days,' she went on to say. 'Then I went back to the nuns and fell apart.'

"There's no mention of my father," added Ben.

Besides little sentences here and there highlighting birthdays and holidays, there were only a few more handwritten entries in the book. One was the morning she had to leave Ben and go back to the orphanage as if he'd never happened. For whatever the reason, the entry was written in the book.

"I didn't sleep last night. How could I?" he read. "After everyone had gone to bed, I snuck down the back stairs to the nursery. There were about twelve babies in there. A few were crying. A few were being fed. My Benny was wrapped in his blanket, sound asleep. Sister Mary Beth knew the nurses. They were nuns. She'd told them about me. So I walked right in. I explained I was leaving in the morning and I wanted to hold my baby. I tried not to cry, but I'm sure any woman would have felt what I felt right then. I'd only been a mother for nine days, yet my whole sense of who I was revolved around this child I'd given birth to, and now I had to hand him over to strangers and forget about him and carry on as if the last nine months existed only in my mind, and that baby—with his spits of hair and dimple on his left cheek and beautiful smile and the ability to make my heart sing and make the world feel hopeful and loving and pure in the purest sense—had to be locked away somewhere within me, as if it were punishment for my sin of passion with the man I fell in love with the first time we met."

Henry walked out of the room. While the wind teased the window panes, Ben waited for him to return and then continued.

"The nurses were very kind. One even embraced me as I pulled myself together. Another put a rocking chair in a small room off to the side and motioned for me to sit down. A few minutes later she came back with my precious baby, a bottle, and a few extra blankets. She told me I could stay as long as I'd like. She shut the door—keeping the world away, at least for a little while. Funny how sometimes our imaginations can kick in without even being asked, for that narrow room, lined with shelves of supplies and one window with the moon looking in became our home. As I sat rocking Benny, and holding his hand, and counting toes, and kissing his perfect little head, and feeling his softness smelling of talcum powder, I imagined we were in our home—safe and sound—and I was rocking him to sleep. I sang to him as he cooed and stretched. I cuddled him as he drank his bottle, and burped him as mothers do, and told him how much I loved him and how I would never forget him. That's when reality smacked me in the head and ripped my heart open even more. If we'd been in our home, I wouldn't be telling my child I'd never forget him. We'd have tomorrow, and tomorrows after that. As I held my Benny close, tears came rolling down my cheeks and on to his blanket. The moon drifted out of sight. Hints of morning took its place. Night was turning into the day I was dreading. I knew it was time to say good-bye, but I couldn't. I kissed his forehead and fingers and toes and angel-like cheeks a million times. He was sleeping when I wrapped him in his blanket. My whole being was screaming quietly as I opened the door of that room and handed him back to the nurse who'd brought him to me. I never looked back. How does a mother ever look back at her child and say good-bye forever? I went up to my room, packed my bag, and waited to be told it was time to go."

There were other entries but Ben chose not to read them. It took a few minutes before anyone could speak, and then the conversation was about some missing photos and not about the entry just read. Sometimes it's better to say nothing, so that's what they did.

"It's obvious six of these pages held photos," said Ben. "Some still have those black triangle corners adhered to them."

"I'd say Sophie took the photos," remarked Ellie. "It would have been a way to keep you with her."

"Why would she leave everything here in boxes?" Andy asked.

"There was so much happening back then," Henry explained. "Orphanages were closing. Sophie was ill. Knowing her like I did, I'm sure she felt this was a safe place for her to leave it. Reality was she had no other option."

"Something tells me your mother made you this teddy bear and quilt," said Ellie, looking inside another box. "The craftsmanship is amazing."

"Sophie was always sewing," Henry said. "Some of the locals would come to the side door of the kitchen with arms full of old clothes for her. That Sophie … she'd take the buttons and zippers off, clean whatever it was—pants, coats—then cut them into pieces of material. She'd braid some for rugs and use the rest for sewing."

"What did she sew?"

"Just about anything, Ellie. She'd stay up late, sewing on her little black Singer. I know she made you a few bears, Ben. I saw them here and there." Henry noticed the snow falling. "We should think about starting back. Snow's already plenty deep for the horses."

If Henry thought it was time, the others listened.

"What do you want to do with the boxes, Ben?"

"A part of me thinks they belong here. It's obvious that's what Sophie wanted."

"I explained your mother had no other option. You do."

"I feel as if I'm disturbing something sacred."

"This place is such a part of you," said Ellie. "It was your second home. These boxes and what's in them belong to you, Ben."

It was a lot to digest. But Ben realized Ellie was right. "I'll take one and leave the rest for another trip."

Ben knew which one he wanted. The other boxes were stacked in the closet. He and Ellie caught up with Henry and Andy, standing in front of Sophie's room.

"I remember one particular stormy, summer night. I can smell the rain," Ben recalled. "I can hear it pounding at the window. The lightning was terrifying. I jumped out of bed and ran in here to be with her. She scooped me up and I fell back to sleep."

Going over to a table sitting under a double window, he explained his mother's sewing machine had sat there. Besides the table, a straight chair, and the bed, the only other furniture was a dresser and a small oak rocker with a quilted seat cover tied around to the back. It was worn right out. A matching pillow was on top of a few boxes piled in a corner. There was no closet. The window was void of curtains.

"No surprises in here," stated Ben, opening one of the boxes. "It's all her sewing stuff."

While Ben checked the other boxes, Ellie rummaged through the one he'd opened first. Spools of thread, boxes of straight pins, and a few pairs of scissors were mingled with remnants of material. One in particular caught her attention. There was something about the woolen plaid. With Henry reminding them they should be going, Ellie didn't have time to figure it out. She put it in her pocket.

"What else did you find, honey?" Ellie asked as they walked back through the kitchen.

Ben didn't answer. He walked past the ovens and went into the larger room where the wind was sending snow mingled with streaks of daylight through cracks in the wall, creating rays of color against the glistening frost. They stood there, amazed at what they were seeing.

"It's like a winter sunset," remarked Andy.

"It's Sophie," explained Henry. "I feel her presence."

Ben stretched out his hand. Opening his fist, he revealed a photo. Though faded, it was obvious that it was of a little boy being rocked in the old oak rocker in the other room by a young woman whose smile could have melted the snow now falling.

Henry put on his gloves and walked outside with Andy right behind.

"You have her smile, Ben." Taking a closer look, Ellie pointed to the photo. "Even though it's hard to see, it's right there—right in the same place as yours. You have your mother's dimple too."

"Slowly, parts are fitting together," said Ben. "A smile, a dimple ... they make sense now. I miss her, Ellie. I feel as if I've always missed her."

"Your mother never said good-bye."

Wrapping Ben up in her arms, Ellie held him close. In the stillness of the moment, bare branches could be heard creaking in the wind.

"There was a piano in here. I'd be dressed in my good clothes and singing with the other boys on Sunday mornings," Ben recalled.

"The piano sat over by the kitchen door," spoke Henry, coming back inside. "Your mother slicked your hair back and had you wear a bow tie, white shirt, and black pants no matter how hot it was."

That was all he could say. That was all anyone could say. With snow-shoes secured, they walked back to the sleigh in silence.

With the sun setting and the wind still blowing, it was colder going back. Goose-down parkas kept them warm as did piles of woolen blankets. The horses never faltered as they led the sleigh through thickets, over creeks, and back out across the fields. Through the pines and hemlocks, the moon was beginning to shed its light, and in the distance church bells sang their soulful song. Pulling the blankets up tighter, Ben held Ellie even closer. Kissing her forehead, he slowly moved his lips to hers as the sleigh that had carried him away had now brought him back to where his journey began. There'd be no stopping him now. The little boy with the dimple would search for his mother. There were no guarantees. But then, there never are.

Chapter Seventeen

Although it had taken a good part of the next day, the tree was finally decorated. After Ben had the lights strung, Ellie took over. That's how they'd done it since living in the upstairs flat near the hospital. Of course, back then, the tree was much smaller. Sometimes it was a table tree.

Andy joined his parents for a late supper. While bowls were filled with barley soup and a spinach salad passed from one to the other, along with bread still warm from the oven, talk was not about gifts yet to buy or presents still to wrap. Rather it was about a family just discovered.

"So you said you aren't practicing tomorrow, Andy?" Ben asked.

"I told the guys I needed a day."

"Don't put them off because of me."

"I'm not. It's because of me. I want to find my grandmother. Last night I did a quick search on those sites you hear advertised, but I hit a dead end each time."

"Sophie may have married or even remarried."

"I thought about that, Mom. Then I googled the last name Beauvais and Sister Mary Beth's convent and what I found was interesting."

Taking a spoonful of soup, he continued. "French Canadians who emigrated here around the 1860s didn't have much money, so most settled in and around New England or in border communities, working on farms or in lumber camps. There was a small cluster of Beauvais' from Quebec who settled in Massachusetts. There may have been more but their last name might have changed when entering the country. I found several leads in Quebec itself, but nothing turned up. Then I remembered her going to a hospital and that, so far, is a dead end. I'll keep trying.

"You mentioned Sister Mary Beth?"

"I remembered Henry saying the convent closed so I kept searching. With other convents also closing, the motherhouse was centralized in western Ohio. It still is. But instead of the eldest nuns living there, they are cared for in retirement facilities around the country. There are five of them. One is about four hours south of here, over the state line. A gentleman donated the property to the nuns. He'd been an orphan."

"Is Sister Mary Beth there?" asked Ben.

"That's the last address I could find for her."

"Is she still alive?"

"It didn't say she wasn't, Dad."

"Print me out directions, Andy. I'll go tomorrow."

"Don't you think you should call first, honey?"

"If Sister Mary Beth has passed away, I'm hoping someone else will remember Sophie ... and me."

"I understand. I'll go with you," said Ellie.

"With Christmas so close, don't feel you have to."

"There's only the three of us, and even if I did have things to finish, which I don't, I'd want to go with you."

Turning to Andy, Ben asked if he'd stay home to give Henry a hand cutting wood. They'd planned on going mid-morning.

"Please don't say where we've gone. If Henry heard any mention of Sister Mary Beth, I'm afraid how he'd react if what we learn isn't what we hope for."

"Are you prepared if that should happen?" Ellie asked.

"I don't know. It's been such a roller coaster. I don't know how I'll react. I'm trying not to go there."

The phone ringing interrupted the conversation.

"If it's Maggie," stated Ben, "Please, no mention of what's going on. It'd be too hard to explain over the phone."

Ellie agreed as she picked up the phone and heard Maggie at the other end. On her way by rail to the Alps, Maggie talked for a good half hour. "I'll call when we get there, Mom." With that, they hung up.

While Andy printed out directions, Ellie cut three pieces of angel food cake and covered them in strawberries while wondering who Maggie was referring to when she said, 'When we get there.' There was something in the way Maggie spoke that led Ellie to think there might be a young man in her daughter's life. Ben was adding a log to the fire when she walked into the front room with the dessert. As she put the serving tray down, her attention was drawn to a nearby window.

"Why does a full moon look fuller this time of year?" she asked.

"Maybe it isn't fuller. Maybe we wish it to be since it's the season of peace on earth and joy and wonder and all the rest."

"Christmas is coming and I don't feel it."

"To be honest, Ellie, I haven't given Christmas a thought. I do know I owe you a weekend in New York."

"Even the stars look bigger, brighter. I should feel it." Ellie hadn't heard a word Ben said. "Think Maggie is remembering Christmases when she was a little girl? I never missed a Christmas at home until we had children."

"The world's a different place, honey. Kids are wired to travel. Jobs that once kept you at a desk are about obsolete. Maggie is young. Her time in Europe will look good on a résumé."

"I get that, but do you think she misses being home? Do you think when she wakes up Christmas morning she'll remember rushing down the front stairs in her nightgown with her braids all which way to see what Santa brought her? Think she'll remember her knitted stocking bulging with little surprises, and leaving cookies and milk for Santa? It always had to be four chocolate-chip cookies on the bone china dish your mother gave me. Think the moon is even fuller in the Alps? Think the stars are bigger, brighter in the Alps?"

"I think," replied Ben, standing behind Ellie and pulling her back to him, "I think Maggie will remember every little thing about every single Christmas spent in this home because you worked so hard to make memories for all of us."

"Why do kids have to grow up?"

"Oh, but Ellie, do any of us ever grow up? We may get old and gray, but when it comes to Christmas, there's still a child within each of us who thinks that yes, the moon is fuller and the stars are bigger and brighter at Christmastime, and yes, Santa needs exactly four chocolate-chip cookies waiting for him on that bone china dish."

A snowplow passing by stopped the questions. Feeling Ben against her, Ellie pulled his arms around her. "I love you, Ben. When I'm afraid, you protect me. When I'm tired, you give me strength. When I worry, you soothe me. See that star? That's the North Star shining down on us."

"I bet it's shining on Maggie, too."

Turning around, Ellie put her arms around Ben's waist and moved her lips to his. It could have led to more, but they stopped abruptly when Andy rushed in.

"You two don't even need mistletoe," he laughed. "Should I leave you alone, or can I eat my cake first?"

"You can stay as long as you eat quickly," joked Ben.

"I can do that, Dad!"

Sitting down, Andy explained the directions he held in his hands.

"How far are we going?" asked Ben.

Sitting by the tree, plans were made and times confirmed as strawberries were enjoyed on a cold and wintry eve. Later on, with Andy back upstairs, Ben took Ellie in his arms and suggested they continue where they'd left off. With violins and a piano setting the mood, as snow drifting down looked like shimmering crystals, the two lovers found pleasure in each other's arms back out on the sun porch. Later, as they were drifting off to sleep, Ben mumbled something about how Ellie could unpack the box full of those little snowmen and put them on the tree if she wanted to.

Ellie was half asleep. She didn't reply.

It was around 2 AM when she sat straight up on the old mattress. She was wide awake.

"That's where I've seen that before," she said under her breath.

Moving quietly out of bed, Ellie put on Ben's flannel that was lying in a chair and tiptoed down the hall to the front closet. After grabbing the piece of material she'd stuffed in her coat pocket when at the summer camp, Ellie fumbled around until finding the box of snowmen sitting on the shelf. Once back in the kitchen, she put the snowmen out on the counter along with the remnant.

"It's a match! I knew I'd seen this material before. The way this piece is cut and the plaid design—they are one and the same."

Some of the snowmen were dressed in it. Some had scarves with frayed edges. Others had little coats or black felt hats trimmed in the plaid.

Ellie kept talking out loud. She had to hear her thoughts to make sense of them.

"Sophie created all these snowmen. I know she did. His father never explained to Ben who'd made them or why he felt it important for Ben to have them along with his adoption papers. It's because Sophie made them."

Ellie took a closer look. It was obvious how much effort went into creating each one. Ellie imagined the young woman in that photo hand-stitching each component and then putting them together and adding a nose and little beady eyes to each one. Their smiles matched, as did the loops on top of their black hats. They were meant to be hung on a Christmas tree.

"That's for another day," Ellie decided. Putting the snowmen back in the box, she shut off the light and tiptoed back down the hall.

Lying in Ben's arms, Ellie moved her fingers through his hair. She loved it when he hadn't shaved for a few days. Sounds of steel strings rambled through her mind as she nibbled at his ear and stroked his neck with a gentle massage. Her presence woke Ben. As the North Star glimmered above, the wind seemed to go in rhythm with the passion on that old pullout sofa. Sometimes love we've grown used to can grow even deeper, no matter what our age, and no matter what the obstacle, even if that obstacle is a box of tattered snowmen sitting on a kitchen counter.

Chapter Eighteen

Despite their best efforts, Ben and Ellie were late getting on the road. Ben blamed it on some wild woman who woke him up in the middle of the night.

It was a clear, cold December day. Ben made up for lost time. In the rush to get going, Ellie hadn't found the time to talk about the snowmen until now.

"Remember mumbling in your sleep about those snowmen you brought home?"

"Vaguely I do. For some reason I was thinking we should hang them on the tree."

"What made you think we should do that?"

"They look like someone spent a lot of time on the details of each one."

"So you like them?"

"You know I go for details and something with a history."

"Sophie made them. Your mother sewed each one by hand and did all the finishing touches."

"How do you know that?"

Ellie admitted to having opened the box of snowmen awhile back. She explained that when she saw that swatch of material packed away in his mother's bedroom, she knew she'd seen it before but couldn't remember where. "When you mumbled something about hanging the snowmen on the tree, that's when I realized where I'd seen it. Some of those snowmen are dressed in it."

"And to think they sat in a closet all those years in the house I grew up in. When we get back home, I'd like to hang them on the tree."

"I realized something else, Ben. When Henry was telling you about that Christmas Eve when he took you in the sleigh to your adopted parents, he explained that you had a bag and a cardboard box with you. Something tells me that the cardboard box is the same cardboard box holding those snowmen. Something also tells me Sophie sent them with you in the sleigh."

Ben was quiet for the rest of the trip.

ANDY'S DIRECTIONS BROUGHT THEM TO THE front door of a sprawling complex called *The Mountain Facility for Sister Elders*. Even though snow covered the grounds, the manicured landscaping was still visible. There were signs for gardens—private, meditating, and flower gardens. One sign pointed to water fountains. No matter which way they looked, the view was spectacular.

Once inside, Ben introduced himself and explained the purpose of his visit. Since they had no appointment, the woman at the front desk made a call to find someone available to speak with them.

"Mr. and Mrs. Paquet," said the receptionist a few minutes later, "right this way."

She led them down a hallway and into a room with a table and chairs in the middle. "Mrs. Felt will be right with you. Please help yourself to coffee. Juice and water are in the refrigerator."

After pouring a half cup, Ellie joined Ben at the table. Before she could take a sip, the social worker was there.

"Welcome to *The Mountain Facility*. I'm Mrs. Felt. I understand you are looking for a nun whom you feel resides with us."

Ben started by saying he'd recently learned he'd been adopted.

"Can you give me what you know?"

"My mother kept me until I was six."

"Do you know where you were born, Mr. Paquet?"

Ben backtracked. He tried to include everything he knew. It didn't take long.

"So you're looking for Sister Mary Beth?"

"Yes."

"I know we have several nuns from that motherhouse, but this is the first I've heard about a summer camp. Come with me. We'll do some searching."

Back in her cubicle, Mrs. Felt explained, "You came on a busy day, Ben. It's our annual Christmas program. Everyone is here."

"I should have called."

"No not at all. Things are just moving a little slower today."

Mrs. Felt pulled up extra chairs for Ben and Ellie. Then she began the process. She had to speak up; the place was full of management types.

"It would help if you could give me more specific information about that summer camp."

Ben started by describing the woods and the surrounding area, down to the river. When he spoke about the orphans sleeping in tents, a rather bald man in a three-piece suit seemed interested. When Ben spoke of Sophie and Sister Mary Beth, the gentleman made it apparent that he was listening.

"Is there something I can help you with, Mr. Webster?"

"I'm sorry, Mrs. Felt. I didn't mean to eavesdrop."

"No problem. This is Ben Paquet and his wife, Ellie. Ben and Ellie, this is Robert Webster, our founder and chairman of the board. Mr. Paquet recently learned he'd been adopted. He was hoping we might be able to help him find some answers."

Instead of shaking Ben's hand, Mr. Webster stood looking at him. A few seconds later, he spoke.

"It is you. You look the same. You still have that impish smile. I helped build a sandbox for you, out alongside the kitchen. You were always with Sophie."

Even though the place was crowded and it was announced over an intercom that the program would begin in an hour, Ben heard nothing except what Mr. Webster was saying.

"I was one of the older orphans. The last I heard about you is how you were adopted on a Christmas Eve. I always felt like an older brother to you. A lot of us did."

Ellie took Ben's hand. That was all Ben needed. "I don't remember much about the orphanage," he said. "It comes back in bits and pieces."

"Some never remember, Ben. Mind if I call you Ben?"

"Not at all."

"You used to call me Bobby. You can still call me Bobby."

"Were you . . ." Ben hesitated. "Were you adopted, Bobby?"

"No, I wasn't. I left the orphanage just before foster care came in."

"Our son told us a man who'd been an orphan was responsible for funding this facility. I never thought our paths might cross."

"You'll learn there's a special bond between orphans. You and I belong to the same family. We shared sleeping spaces. We shared a place to eat. Most often the only thing orphan families don't share is the same last name."

"How did you go from there to here?"

"We were taught the value of hard work. I eventually opened my own investment firm. But I never forgot where I came from, Ben. I never forgot those who grew up beside me, and you were one of them."

"But I don't remember anyone."

"Give it time. You were a little guy when you were adopted. Up to that point, Sophie kept you pretty much by her side."

Ben's reaction to Bobby's remark didn't go unnoticed.

"Would you and your wife like to sit down with me in my office?" Webster asked. "It's a little more private there."

A few minutes later they were sitting in leather chairs facing one wall covered in plaques and awards earned by Mr. Robert Webster who explained, "I know Mrs. Felt introduced me as founder and chairman of the board. I prefer no title. I feel that those who've attained success have a responsibility to give back. That's what this is all about." He paused. "How can I help?"

Ben explained that he was searching for Sister Mary Beth.

"Sister Mary Beth was a favorite nun. I've had many an inquiry about her over the years. She took good care of all of us."

"She's passed away?"

"Although quite frail and confused, Sister Mary Beth is still with us."

"Here?"

"Yes. Right now she's probably being brought into the auditorium."

"Would I be able to speak with her? I wouldn't be long."

"I'm certain you can see her. I don't guarantee how coherent she'll be. Every day is different."

"I'd like to at least try. It's important that I try."

Once again Bobby sensed urgency in Ben's words. "Maybe I can answer some of your questions. Sister Mary Beth has confided in me over the years. She once told me she felt like a mother to all of us. Anything you say remains between us. You know, for your age, you were a pretty good ball boy. I always chose you for my team."

"Why?"

"Why did I choose you?"

"No. Why didn't you ever get adopted?"

"I was an overweight kid. Maybe anyone who checked me out thought I'd eat too much. Who knows, Benny? It wasn't meant to be. How'd adoption work out for you?"

"I had a good home and good parents."

"I hear reservation in your voice."

"I never could put my finger on it growing up. My adopted mother and father made sure I had anything I needed. They were there for me, but somewhere inside I felt something was missing."

"No need to explain. It goes with the territory."

"Do you keep in touch with any of the orphans?"

"Yes, I do. Over the years I've built an extensive database of those who lived at the orphanage. Many live in the Northeast. Quite a few live in your area."

Bobby paused to answer the phone; he continued a few minutes later. "I wondered what happened to you and Sophie. She took good care of you. I figured it was because you were the youngest. Do you remember her?"

Ben heard the words roll off his tongue. He couldn't stop them. "About Sophie... Sophie's why I'm here."

From that moment on, the little boy was back. "I learned I was adopted when my father was on his deathbed. He didn't have much to say after he handed me my adoption papers. It was through an older gentleman whom I've known for a long time that I learned the details of my first six years. He told me about my birth parents."

"That's pretty heavy stuff. I used to imagine my birth parents' names. I don't do that anymore."

"You don't want to know who they were, or where they lived, or why they gave you up?"

"I decided after I'd worked my way through college that it no longer mattered. I was comfortable with who and what I'd become. How do you feel now that you have actual names and some history?"

"I want to know more. That's why I'm here. Sister Mary Beth knew my mother." Ben hesitated for a second. "And so did you, Bobby."

Tapping a pencil on his desk, Bobby pushed his chair back. He stood and walked over to the window. "When I try to figure things out, I stand here and marvel at what I see. I don't have to stand here today. It all makes sense now. Sophie took you under her wing because she was your mother." Turning around, he added. "You have her dimple, Benny."

After Bobby made a call to see if Sister Mary Beth was settled in, Ben told more of his story. As they walked up the hallway and into the auditorium, Bobby Webster pledged his support in helping Benny find the answer he most wanted to know: Was his mother still alive?

Chapter Nineteen

Decorated in fresh boughs and wreaths with red velvet bows, the auditorium was at near full capacity. With the program open to the public, Bob explained it was always well attended. A state-of-the-art sound system made it seem as if Bing Crosby was up on the stage.

"We plan for this event all year," he said. "The highlight is the unveiling of the tree. You're welcome to stay."

"Thanks. We'd love to," replied Ben, taking hold of Ellie's hand.

An announcement interrupted the music, telling everyone they should be seated. The crowd was buzzing! Bob hurried along as he spoke. "I see her. Over there!"

Working his way down the aisle to behind one particular wheelchair, he asked Ben and Ellie to wait. Going around to the front, Bob got down on one knee.

"Sister Mary Beth. It's Bobby. You have some visitors. They've come a long way to see you." Turning to Ben, he said, "She's waking up. Come around by me."

Ben waited as Sister Mary Beth slowly lifted her head and opened her eyes.

"Get closer."

Ben did as Bob suggested. He looked directly at the old woman who had been the young woman making arrangements for so many adoptions. Bob had explained how she'd pray for guidance with every placement.

Clearing his throat, Ben tried to speak, but he couldn't. It turned out, he didn't have to as Sister Mary Beth lifted her hand to his. Ben took hold. Looking into her eyes, images from that night before Christmas flashed through his mind. He remembered the snow falling, and the sleigh stopping, and the warmth of Sister Mary Beth hugging him tightly. Then she disappeared into the night, leaving Ben alone and on his way to his new home, wondering why she'd been crying when it was supposed to be a happy time, and wondering why she didn't go with him as she had with the others. With tears streaming down her cheeks, Sister Mary Beth brought his hand over her heart. Despite the chatter and singing in the room, she spoke over it. It was apparent that she was determined to be heard as she motioned for him to move even closer.

"My little Benny. My little Benny," she repeated. Reaching up, she pulled him tight, hugging him and kissing the top of his head. Her hands outlined his face as she kept saying his name.

"I've kept you in my prayers, my Benny, since saying good-bye that Christmas Eve. I should have stayed with you. I should have stayed."

As Sister Mary Beth wiped away her tears, Ben told her he understood. He thanked her for finding him a good home.

"Sit by me. Tell me where life has taken you, my boy." She kept hold of his hand. Her smile made it feel like summer.

After Ben introduced Ellie, Bob cleared space for them to sit down. Then Ben filled her in with as many details as possible until the curtain opened.

Although the program lasted less than an hour, Ellie told Ben she considered this the Broadway show they hadn't seen.

"The music was exceptional—the chorus, breathtaking," she added.

But the best came at the end when the curtain was drawn and the lights dimmed. It was very quiet until a faint ringing of handbells and the innocence of young voices filled the auditorium.

From nowhere came children walking down the center aisle and up onto the stage. The boys were dressed in white shirts, red ties, and black pants. The girls were in long-sleeved white blouses and black skirts, with red ribbons in their hair. Each was carrying a candle and singing "Silent Night." As the bells rang and the snow fell, the curtain rose to reveal the splendor of a Christmas tree. Strands and strands of tiny white lights illuminated the branches. Pulling his hand over her heart again, Sister Mary Beth pointed to the tree. She pulled Ben near.

"Take a closer look," she insisted.

Ben did as she asked. The tree was truly breathtaking. Antique ornaments and glass bulbs in reds and greens were hanging amidst strings of glittering snowflakes and tiny pearls. As a critic of detail, Ben felt the tree was one of the most beautifully decorated trees he'd ever seen. Sister Mary Beth kept pointing. She urged him to get closer. So he did.

With the chorus singing and the audience clapping, Ben walked up to the front of the stage as a spotlight from up in the balcony focused directly on the tree. That's when Ben understood what Sister Mary Beth was trying to say. Woven about the antique ornaments, glass bulbs, and glittering snowflakes, he found little snowmen of all sizes, dressed in remnants, with sweet smiles and dots of black for eyes, all hung in place by simple loops of thread. Ben lost count of how many there were. He understood what Sister Mary Beth was telling him. That's why a few minutes later, Ben took a wrinkled photo from his wallet and showed it to her.

"Is my mother still alive Sr. Mary Beth?"

Ben thought she'd answered yes, but she'd fallen asleep.

"This is her nap time," explained the aide.

"I understand. Does she have many visitors?"

"Yes, mostly adults she's placed in homes over the years. They come to say thank you, or to try to gain information on their birth parents."

"Have you ever seen an older woman around her age?"

Bob interrupted. "If Sophie had been here, Ben, I would have noticed. I daresay not even the passing of time could have diminished her beauty. It was inside her, you know."

"Does she receive packages?"

"I'd have to check on that," said Bob. "What is it that you are trying to figure out?"

As Sister Mary Beth was being wheeled out of the auditorium, Ben explained about the snowmen and how certain he was that Sophie had made them. Ellie added her story about the remnant.

"I was thinking that if Sister Mary Beth had received any of them recently," added Ben, "then that would mean Sophie is still alive."

"I can check on that for you, Ben. We keep track of everything that comes in here." Walking over to the stage, Bob took a closer look at the tree. "Those snowmen, right? Those are the ones you are referring to?"

"Yes. When my father told me I was adopted, he handed me a box full of them."

Bob stood back in amazement. "Now that I take a closer look, I realize I have snowmen like these on my tree. I've had them for years. I can't tell you where they came from. My kids had names for them. They'd play with them under the tree. I can't believe I never noticed them here before. I think there's more of a meaning to these snowmen than we realize. I'll post some inquiries to that database I told you about. We'll find your answers, Ben. That's what family is about."

It was snowing when they started back. Plows were out. The wind was whipping across the highway.

"Instead of stopping for dinner, I think we should head straight home, Ellie. This snow doesn't look like it will let up."

"Whatever you think, Ben. You must be exhausted after today."

"More than I expected. Both Sr. Mary Beth and Bobby were helpful, but I still have more questions than answers."

"I was encouraged by the database Bobby's put together. That, to me, could prove valuable in your search for Sophie."

"I agree. One thing I don't understand, though, is why Bobby has no interest in finding his family when he helps others find theirs."

"When you think about it, Ben, all he ever knew was the orphanage."

Four hours later they were in the kitchen, eating sloppy joes Andy had made. He told his parents what a great day he'd had with Henry.

"We didn't chop wood. Instead, Henry hitched up the sleigh, and we went back to the camp."

"What prompted you to do that?" Ben asked.

"Henry thought it was a perfect day to go pick up your boxes. We put them in the carriage house."

"That's a good, dry place. I can go through them whenever I get the time."

"That's what Henry said."

"Did you miss the snowstorm?"

"We were lucky, Dad. We made it out of the woods just as it started."

"Did you go in on snowshoes?" Ellie asked.

"No. Henry led the horse's right to the front door. The snow was powder, so we flew!"

"I can't imagine how breathtaking the ride in must have been, with the trees and fields," Ellie added.

"Henry told me how Sophie used to paint scenes from down there. He said they were pretty good."

"Now we know my mother was also a painter. This is another piece of her puzzle."

Andy abruptly changed the subject. "I got an email today saying the tour starts the end of January with a gig through Europe."

"Are you sure about this, Andy?"

"I'm sure, Dad. One of my professors called to ask what I'd decided. He told me to keep in touch. He said I could always take courses online."

"He must like you, Andy, to call you."

"He's a good guy. One day in class, he told us he'd quit college years back, after his first semester. He had this thing that he wanted to play baseball in the major leagues."

"So what happened?"

"He was a pitcher—made it to the minors and was getting noticed until taking a ball head-on. He never did get back to where he needed to be to play at that next level, but he told us that if he hadn't tried, he would never be satisfied with where he is today. He believes it boils down to going with your gut. What he said makes me think of you, Dad. My gut tells me Sophie is alive."

"My gut tells me the crowds will love you, Andy!"

"Let's hope so, Dad." After saying good night, Andy went up the stairs with his phone to his ear.

It was close to eleven when Ellie brought the box of snowmen into the front room. With the fire crackling, Ben hung each one, way back in, on branches surrounded by glittering ornaments and those scribbled with crayons.

"They made it home, Ellie."

"So have you, Ben."

"That's because of you, my love."

They sat by the fire late into the night as little snowmen dressed in worn cloth took their places on the tree in the front room of the old stone home. Sometimes it's the simple things that mean the most. They don't have to be wrapped in fancy boxes. Wrapped in love will do just fine.

Chapter Twenty

Ellie thought she had her baking done until learning of a family in need. They'd lost everything in a fire a few days earlier. For some unknown reason she was drawn to their story. With two children, the need was great, so Ellie was baking cookies for them. She'd weeded through Maggie's closet back in the fall. The bags of clothing were still sitting where she'd left them, waiting to be taken somewhere. Now they had a purpose. The newspaper had given sizes. They'd probably fit the mother. Besides baking cookies, Ellie had gone to the store and played Santa. Once Ben got back, she'd ask him to go with her. She'd wrapped the gifts in Santa paper. *Every child deserves presents wrapped in Santa paper,* she told herself.

Sitting at the table, getting ready to pack cookies in a box, Ellie looked around the kitchen and through the doorway, down the hall, to the front stairway. Except for the dripping faucet, the house was still. It was hard to believe Christmas was but a few days away. Ben would remind her again how things change.

"Kids grow up, and there's nothing you can do but to go along with it," he'd say.

While she knew he was right, there were times, like this, that she missed it all. It wasn't the gifts, but rather the anticipation. She used to tell herself she'd be glad when the kids were older. With age comes wisdom, and sitting there, she confessed she'd give anything to greet slippered feet hurrying down those stairs on Christmas morning.

Hearing Ben pull up, she thought of his Christmases in the orphanage. She wondered how Sophie had kept her secret to herself. How could she have tucked him in bed on Christmas Eve without telling him how much his mommy loved him? How could she resist scooping him up in her arms on Christmas morning and telling him Santa had left her little boy presents wrapped in special paper? She must have loved him very much to be able to let him go, she decided.

Even before walking through the door, Ben knew Ellie was making cookies. The sweet aroma of melted chocolate and brown sugar had drifted out beyond the hemlocks lining the driveway.

"I thought you were through baking?"

"I was Ben, until I read the paper."

Ellie told him about the family and why she was baking. "I read the story over and over trying to imagine losing everything. Making it worse, it's Christmas and that family has two little boys. All I have left to do is finish boxing the cookies," she said.

Ben didn't hesitate. "I'm with you, honey." He packed the car while Ellie layered the cookies in wax paper. They were on the road a few minutes later, heading some twenty-five miles away.

"I haven't been out this way in years," said Ben, making a left onto a country road that would take them through one-street hamlets and small towns once supported by thriving farms. As with other parts of the country, much of the landscape had changed, leaving the little villages to fend for themselves. Downtowns, once busy with mom-and-pop stores, were struggling. Places were boarded up. It was obvious that the ones still surviving were on thin ice.

"It's beautiful out here with the fields smothered in snow and a few cornstalks still standing," said Ellie, "I feel closer to Christmas, if that makes any sense."

"It makes perfect sense," Ben said. "Being surrounded by this countryside stirs the soul. Sadly, some of the farms around this area have been deserted. Henry was saying earlier today that he'd read how high the loss in tax revenue is because of abandoned properties."

"I don't understand how you can pack up your belongings and walk out the front door. Every one of these places is a tragedy."

"I look at them as untold stories of families, Ellie."

Ben slowed down. "Look over there, at that farm. There's a swing in the tree. Curtains are hanging in a few of the windows not boarded up. It makes me wonder who they were; how many kids played on that swing?"

"It's haunting, Ben. It looks like they'll be back. They mustn't have had any other options."

"Vacating a homestead would not be an option for me," said Ben. "I'd fight tooth and nail to keep it. I'd put a plan together right down to the last penny. I'm not judging these people, Ellie. I realize there are many variables involved, and making such a decision is personal."

"You're a man of detail, honey. Without details, you're not the architect. Without details, you'll never know that little boy who rode in the back of a sleigh on Christmas Eve. I understand that. For some like Bobby, it doesn't matter."

Ellie could tell Ben was thinking. She wondered if he'd heard anything she'd said. And then she noticed a tear—and then another falling from his eyes as he took her hand, driving by more of those empty homes.

"You get me, Ellie."

"Down to your core, I get you, Ben."

Except for the wind stretching across the road, it was quiet for a few miles. Fences once in the distance came into full view and then rambled back out of sight. A sign nailed to a wooden post told them their destination wasn't far. Letting go of Ellie's hand to maneuver a sharp turn, Ben broke the silence.

"Mind if I ask Henry to dinner on Christmas Eve again this year, Ellie? He seems down. I can't figure him out. He's never down."

"I'd planned on him. We can go to church in the morning. There's no Santa rush to keep us up half the night. No impossible instructions to follow, because there are no toys to put together."

"There's something about Christmas, isn't there? We look back more than we look forward. That must be what Henry is doing. I know he misses Helen. But it's deeper than that."

Taking Ellie's hand again, Ben added, "And I know you're missing Maggie. So am I, honey. Our little girl has grown up."

Once through a village resembling the 1800s, the road narrowed even more.

"According to the paper," said Ellie, "the community where our family lives has provided them with a home for Christmas."

"It reminds me of Bobby talking about the orphanage and how those of us who lived there shared everything but the same last name. We were a community inside that orphanage."

"It's heartwarming when a community reaches out. I wasn't going to bake cookies. I was going to run to the grocery, but then I remembered how Maggie and Andy labored over every sugar cookie they chose. Suddenly it was as if those two little boys were our two little ones."

Ben took a left which led them to what looked like a once-busy downtown. It was only one street but it showcased buildings that caught Ben's eye.

"It'd cost a fortune to build these today. Look up toward the tops. See the scrolled designs? The brickwork is an art form of long ago. Those inset windows are priceless."

"It's sad to see so many closed."

"One thing for sure—they won't decay unless there's water damage, and with those tin roofs, that's not going to happen."

"There's our turn, Ben, just before the bridge."

Taking the right led them to a street lined with towering oaks and Victorian homes. Some had wraparound verandas. Most had wreaths on their doors and decorations in their yards, except for the address they were seeking. When Ben pulled up, the two children sitting on the front porch bundled in snowsuits ran inside. Seconds later a young woman dressed in jeans and a heavy sweater with her hair pulled back off her shoulders walked out of the door and down the steps with the children following behind her. She seemed to realize why these two strangers had stopped as she made her way along the sidewalk towards them.

Ben stepped out of the car and found himself hugging the woman and telling her that everything would work out. Christmas has a way of bringing lost souls together.

"We felt we had to come," Ben explained. "We're here to support you and your family."

After the introductions, Ellie grabbed the box of cookies on the back seat.

"Something tells me you boys like cookies. I made these for you."

Taking the top off, she offered the children a cookie. One of the boys reached in and took one. The other studied every cookie in the box.

"Picking out the right cookie is important. Our son used to take forever and when he did choose one, he'd lick the frosting off before eating it."

"That's what I do," said the boy, picking one up and licking the frosting until it was gone. Then he devoured it and took another.

"When I read of your loss, Mrs. Bailey," explained Ellie, "I put myself in your shoes. I can't begin to comprehend how you must feel."

"I'm still counting my blessings. What we lost can be rebuilt. Please, call me Susan."

"Mommy, we lost Tinker. Remember, Tinker died."

"Yes. I'm sorry, Matt. Of course I remember we lost Tinker. Maybe Santa will bring you a new kitten."

"But Santa doesn't know where we live."

"Santa knows, honey. That's why he has his elves."

Matt seemed satisfied with his mother's answer—or it could have been the cookies. Asking if he could have another, he then ran into the house.

"The boys are convinced Santa will go to the home we lost and when he doesn't find them there, he'll move on to the next family on his list. My husband and I keep telling them that Santa will come but they have their doubts."

"Something tells me you'll convince them, Susan," said Ben, his arms full of bagged clothes.

Once inside, he put them down with other bags from so many other strangers.

"We're overwhelmed by the generosity shown us," Susan explained.

"Despite what you hear in the news, Susan, the human spirit is alive and well."

"You're right, Ben. Please. Sit down. My husband is due back any minute."

"We don't want to keep you," said Ellie.

"Oh, you're not. We're waiting to put the Christmas tree up!"

"When is Daddy coming?"

"Any minute, Matt."

A box full of photos sitting near the sofa caught Ellie's attention. "I see you were able to save some pictures, Susan."

"If we'd lost them, we would have lost our story in photos."

Looking at the box, Ben understood what those various sized frames holding pictures represented. He had one photo of his mother—one priceless photo.

The other boy, a bit younger than Matt, picked up one of the framed photos and brought it to his mother. He was limping.

"This is Billy," said Susan. "Billy's our hero. He woke us up that night. He hurt his leg when he jumped out our bedroom window. But it's getting better."

"Show that man my picture, Mommy."

"You show him, Billy. The man's name is Ben."

The little boy wasn't shy. He sat down with Ben and talked about the picture. It was Billy with his great-grandfather, holding up a line of fish.

"My Gramps was a great fisherman. He told me stories."

"What kind of stories? Dinosaurs and dragon stories?"

"No. He told stories about when he was a little boy and lived in a big house with lots of other kids. I liked his stories."

"Did you and your Gramps go fishing a lot?"

"Yes! That's when he told me stories about when he'd go fishing a long time ago with a bunch of kids. He was lucky. He camped out in tents. They were big tents, Gramps said."

The front door opened. Billy jumped off Ben's lap and joined his brother.

"Do we have our stuff to put on the tree, Daddy?"

"Yes, Matt, we have all the decorations. Do you two want to help me bring the tree in off the porch?" asked the tall, young man giving his sons a hug.

It only took a few minutes. Watching them reminded Ellie of when Andy was their age. He'd tug and pull the tree right alongside Ben. He followed in his father's footsteps even back then.

After the tree was situated, Susan introduced her husband, Will, to Ben and Ellie, telling him of their generosity.

"People like you continue to amaze us," said Will.

"We came because we wanted to help. There are still gifts to be brought inside, but," said Ellie in a whisper, "they're meant for Christmas morning."

"Thank you again," replied Will.

"When can we put the tree up?"

"We'll put the tree up later, right in front of that big window, Matt."

"Do we have enough stuff to put on it? Did all our stuff burn in the fire, too?"

"Daddy told you both we have our decorations, Matt."

"I want to see them," said Billy.

After explaining how Billy was having nightmares since the fire, Susan went out on the front porch. She came back carrying a big box. "Here are the decorations, boys. Be careful with them. Some are pretty old."

Continuing where she'd left off, Susan told Ellie how they'd talked with a counselor. "He suggested we keep stressing the fact that they are safe and how everything they once knew isn't lost forever."

Laughter diverted Susan's attention to the boys. "Remember I said be careful. Take the decorations out one at a time."

"I can only imagine how frightening that fire was for all of you."

"I still feel the heat of the flames," Susan explained. "The smoke was suffocating. I'm convinced we were being watched over that night."

"Billy claims his Gramps woke him up," added Will. "They were very close. We lost him last year. Billy talks about him all the time."

"I would like to ask you something, Will, and if it is none of my business, tell me. I realize you don't even know us, but I believe there's yet another reason for our being here today." Ben paused before continuing, "Was your ... was your grandfather an orphan?"

"Yes, he was. What led you to believe he'd been an orphan?"

"As Billy was telling me about your grandfather living in a big house with lots of other kids, going fishing and camping out in tents, I knew what your son was describing. Everything he talked about was a part of my childhood, too."

Ben's input led to Will talking about his grandfather. "He was a proud man. He built a good life. Gramps married my grandmother when he was eighteen. 'Fresh out of the orphanage,' he'd say, 'and into the arms of the love of my life.' They had a large family. He'd often say he wanted his children to grow up surrounded by siblings like he did. He considered the other orphans his brothers and sisters. He said that gave him a sense of belonging which he felt shaped his life in a good way. He farmed a big spread up until a week before he died—exactly five months after my grandmother passed away. His heart was broken when he lost her. Anyway, Gramps gave each of us a parcel of land a while back. He wanted us to have homes because he never did. That's where our place was located."

"Gramps received letters from other orphans, didn't he Will?" asked Susan.

"He did. He received several letters over the years. He loved getting the letters. That's when he'd go on about a summer camp which is where he started fishing."

"I was at that camp until I was six. That's where those tents were pitched."

"Gramps would tell us they'd bring their catch to a pretty young girl. She'd cook the fish and serve them for dinner. He spoke of her often—of how kind she was to them. I think he had a crush on her. They probably were about the same age from what he said."

"Did your grandfather get letters from her?" asked Ben.

"He received so many, Ben."

"Look Mommy," interrupted Billy. "The snowmen are chasing the reindeer."

"Please don't do that, honey. Those snowmen are very old."

Ben knew before he looked that the snowmen wore little smiles, had dots for eyes, and were dressed in woolen remnants. He felt them near. From somewhere, he heard a lullaby being sung to him. It had been raining. Wrapped in a blanket, he was being rocked on a small porch by someone smelling of Ivory soap and cinnamon. Her voice was soft. Her fingers moved his hair off his forehead as she sang. The hustle of others scurrying by didn't stop her as she whispered to him how much his mommy loved him; telling him he'd forever be her little boy. Someone interrupted her, but only for a moment. She replied that his fever was down. Pulling him closer, she told him there was a rainbow.

"You always bring me rainbows," she whispered. Then she sang her little boy to sleep.

Before Ben could say a word, Billy was back in his lap. As the conversation continued, one little boy played and pretended with snowmen made by another little boy's mother many years ago.

Chapter Twenty-One

"YOU ASKED IF MY GRANDFATHER RECEIVED letters from that particular young woman, Ben."

"I have to be honest with you, Will. I'm curious if she ever wrote to him because I recently learned she is my birth mother. But that's about all I know about her."

"I am happy for you, Ben," remarked Will. "Problem is I can't say if they made it out of the fire or if they were even in the house. Before he died, my grandfather asked if I'd help him put the letters in order. By the time we were through, the letters were organized in a file."

"Do you remember where that file was kept, honey?"

"It's not in the garage, Susan. I've been back several times since the fire."

"I don't remember seeing it in the house," added Susan.

"That leaves my grandfather's place. I'll give my brother a call. He moved in after Gramps died."

Will was back a few minutes later. "He has the file. Let's go get it and you can take it home with you, Ben."

"How wonderful the file is safe. I'm happy for you, too, Ben," said Susan. "I remember listening to Will's grandfather talking about trying to find his birth parents when he was younger. He got as far as where he was born, but that's where the trail ended, right Willie?"

"That's right. A fire destroyed any records that would have helped him continue his search."

"How ironic," said Ellie. "One fire stops a search; another may hopefully start one."

"The only way we'll know is if we get those letters," Susan said.

"Who wants to go to Gramps?" Will asked.

Both the boys jumped up. Billy asked Ben if he could ride with him.

"That's up to your mom and dad, Billy."

"It's fine with us. We only have a few miles to go," said Susan.

After sneaking presents into the house, they were ready. Billy sat next to Ben and talked all the way. Some of what he said was about the night of the fire. Ben and Ellie let him talk. They didn't interrupt with questions. Ben told him how brave he was to have saved his family.

"But Tinker died."

"Tinker loves you, Billy," said Ben, "He knows you did your best."

"Is Tinker with my Gramps?"

"Yes. They're together, Billy."

"They're probably out fishing."

"Do cats like to fish?" Ben asked. "I thought they ate fish."

"Tinker did both!"

Once they reached the old farmhouse, the boys were up the front steps in seconds. Will introduced his brother John to Ellie and Ben.

"Please, come in," said John. "I put the file on the kitchen table."

"I can't thank you both enough. I'll bring the letters back soon."

"There's no hurry. I'm sure you're busy, like everyone else," said Will.

After a good half hour sitting around the table, Ben noticed the time. He suggested to Ellie they get on the road.

Thanking them again, Ben turned to the boys. "You two get to bed early Christmas Eve. I'm certain you're first on Santa's list."

Billy was fighting back tears. Giving Ben a hug, Billy told him he'd take care of the snowmen.

Ben was surprised by Billy's remark. He couldn't help but ask why he'd said it.

"I saw how you looked at them. You like them just like I do. If you want to go fishing, we can go in Gramps's boat."

"I'll remember that, Billy. I used to go fishing with my little boy."

"He can come too."

Although they'd only met a few hours ago, Ben felt close to the little boy who'd saved his family. That might have been the reason why.

As the moon shed its light over snow-covered cornstalks, Ben and Ellie headed back, with letters waiting to be read.

Chapter Twenty-Two

"I DIDN'T HEAR YOU COME IN last night, Andy."

"It was late, Dad."

"Good practice?"

"It was after we got going."

Sitting down at the table, Andy asked his father a question, but Ben didn't answer. He was distracted by a pile of letters.

"I'm sorry, Andy. What did you say?"

"I asked where all these letters came from."

Getting up for another cup of coffee, Ben told him about the day before.

"There might be letters from your mother?"

"There could be, Andy."

"Good morning." With three days to go before the twenty-fifth and a Christmas menu to check one last time, Ellie couldn't sleep. It didn't matter that there'd only be four gathered to celebrate the holiday.

"How's the search going, honey?"

"Slow. I get pulled into every letter I open."

"I'm sure each has a story to tell, Ben."

"While each is unique, they're all the same. They want to connect. They're seeking answers. Some are written by orphans. Others come from family members looking for orphans."

Minutes later Ellie was scrambling eggs and toasting bagels as Ben kept opening envelopes.

He lost track of time. Sometimes he'd make a remark. Other times he'd sit there, oblivious to what was going on around him. Ellie served the eggs and bagels without saying a word. She called the butcher about the turkey, gathered bowls and china, and brought out the good silver. She started making a list, which surprised her, because she thought she had made her last trip to the store. But when it comes to Christmas, she decided, no one is ever ready. A knock at the door caught Ellie cleaning carrots.

Andy was on his way out the front door to shovel. "I'll get it, Mom," he shouted.

Seconds later, he was back in the kitchen carrying two boxes. "The big one's from Maggie." Looking at the postmark, Andy told his mother that the other one was from her cousin's husband.

"I told Maggie she didn't have to do that," Ellie said. "Leave them on the dining room table, Andy. I'll deal with them later."

Greasing cake pans used every Christmas for as long as Ellie could remember, her thoughts went back to a Christmas growing up with that particular cousin. It was a few nights before Christmas Eve. They lived side by side out in the country, and that evening was like so many other winter evenings. The moon was breathtaking, lighting the way as they skated around the frozen creek which etched a pathway through the fields. There must have been a zillion dazzling stars adding to the splendor. Later they lay atop the ice and talked about a family recipe. Remembering the conversation, Ellie looked over at Ben, searching for a connection that had molded him into the man she loved. That innocent conversation, spoken years ago between best of cousins waiting for Christmas, put meaning to his pain in a simple way. It was her cousin who'd made the first statement that started it all.

"Mom told me our grandmother used to make the same Christmas bread she makes every year for Christmas breakfast. It's a secret family recipe!"

"How can it be secret if they all know it? My mother makes it too."

"It's kept in the family. Mom said it started a very long time ago."

"So we can use it?"

"Yes, because we are family. But we have to keep it secret."

"We can't tell anybody, Abbey?"

"We can only tell people in our family."

"I can't tell Bonnie's mother? Bonnie is my best friend."

"Bonnie is not family. You can't tell her, Ellie."

Ellie never told Bonnie's mother. She did hand it down to Maggie when she was old enough to appreciate it. Maggie never shared the recipe, even when she made it for her European colleagues. She explained it was a family recipe. *Abbey would be proud of her,* thought Ellie.

Ellie's favorite cousin had passed away a few years back. Ellie still couldn't believe it. They'd been so close. They'd stayed in touch. Now Ellie made sure she stayed in touch with Abbey's husband. *There's something about Christmas and the memories it stirs of loved ones no longer with us,* she thought. She remembered the package he'd sent, now sitting on the dining room table. When the house was quiet, she decided that's when she would open it.

Andy was back inside and Ellie had the cake cooling when Ben told them almost in a whisper that he'd found one envelope with perfect penmanship. That's all he said. He sat there staring at it. His face turned white, his hands were shaking. Ben knew who it was from. He knew it. He'd seen that penmanship before.

"Ben! Are you OK?" Ellie sat down next to him. Andy sat on the other side.

"This is from my mother. I feel her. She's near just as she was when it stormed and she protected me and when I was sick, she comforted me. It's from my mother."

Shifting the envelope around in his hands, Ben noted that the letter had never been opened. "It was mailed last year. It must have been after Will's grandfather passed away."

"Dad, that means she was still alive! What's the postmark?"

Taking a closer look, Ben could see that it came from Portsmouth.

"She lived in Portsmouth, Ellie! How many times have we been through there! I wonder if our paths ever crossed."

"We could go today, Dad!"

"Go where? There's no return address."

"Maybe there are clues in the letter as to where she lives," suggested Ellie.

"That doesn't mean she's still there or that she's still alive."

"You're right. But it's a start, Ben."

"All you need is a start," Andy added.

Ben slowly opened the envelope. He had so many questions as he started to read a letter signed by his mother not very long ago.

My dear Paul,

While years have passed, I haven't forgotten you or any of the orphans who asked me to cook their fish! Yes, it's me—the girl who had the pleasure of cooking for you and other great fishermen down at the summer camp. I look back at that time in my life with joy in my heart—with memories made more precious by each passing day. On occasion I have run into others who also called that place home.

Such an occasion happened last week. I was sitting in my shop, cutting fabric, with the Dutch door open to catch the breeze off the ocean—something this old lady does even when the weather turns cold and the cobblestones are covered with snow. So engrossed was I in the task at hand that I didn't hear people coming in. It was the clock on the square ringing out the noon hour that caught my attention. Since I'd planned on going over there for clam chowder, I made my way to the front of the shop, only to discover those people browsing. It was a couple. She was a seamstress, too. The bolts of fabric and the old Singer in the window had caught her eye. We got to talking. One thing led to another, and wouldn't you know, the gentleman had been with us in the orphanage. In fact, Paul, he says he keeps in touch with you. He even stopped by your farm one summer and visited with you. His name is Lawrence. You boys called him Larry the Fairy back then. I can't believe the nuns never heard you! Anyway, it is through Lawrence that I learned your dear wife passed away earlier in the year.

I am writing to tell you how sorry I am for your loss. I've al-

ways felt a sense of pride when those of us who shared our lives together went out into the world and found our way, with our feet firmly planted and our sense of self ready to embrace whatever life presented. You did that, Paul. By all accounts, you were a loving husband. You remain a caring father—and while that role changes over the years, it never goes away. Being a parent is both a gift and a challenge. Sometimes decisions we make stay with us all our lives and tug at our hearts every day.

I will keep you and your family in my prayers, my dear friend. If you'd ever like to visit, please do. I'm busiest when fall leads to the holidays. I just can't keep the trees full of those little snowmen. I'll send more soon.

The letter was simply signed *Sophie.*

Ben's thoughts took him to New Hampshire and that little shop with the old Singer and the bolts of fabric in the window. He wasn't alone. Ellie and Andy were thinking the same thing.

"We have to go, Dad."

"Believe me, Andy, it's all I can do to keep from jumping in the truck. But we have to think this through."

"How can we help, honey?" asked Ellie.

"I need to call Bobby. I want to ask him about Lawrence."

Ben tried Bobby's cell phone. Seconds later they were talking. Bobby remembered Lawrence. In fact, Lawrence was in his database.

"Larry keeps in touch, Ben. The number I have for him is current. Keep me informed."

Seconds later Ben was dialing a man who might have the answers he needed. After getting through the introduction, Ben explained how he got his number. Although Ben had been a lot younger, Lawrence remembered the little kid who was "Sophie's favorite."

"That's why I'm calling, Lawrence. I understand you and your wife ran into Sophie in New Hampshire. I'm heading that way myself and would love to connect with her."

There was a pause at the other end. Ben felt his heart in his throat. He was afraid of what Lawrence was going to say next.

"My wife and I enjoy traveling through New England in late fall. After having stumbled upon Sophie the year before, we made it a point to include her in our stops this time around. My wife fell in love with her shop. The two of them talked fabric and sewing for over an hour. Sophie was quite generous with her time, despite being in the middle of a project. She had bits of material stacked all over the place, yet she took time to make us a cup of tea. We were anticipating another enjoyable visit with her, but when we arrived, the door was locked. The lights were out and the curtains drawn. Taped to the front door was a sign saying the shop was closed due to illness. That's all it said. No number was given—no date when she might be back."

Ben asked when they'd been there.

"We always block off the first two weeks in October. My wife doesn't like driving in snowstorms, and they have some pretty bad ones."

Ben asked for directions, explaining that it was "in case I decide to go at some point."

Lawrence added, "Because the Christmas tree was in the front window, we figured she'd been there. It was full of little snowmen as it had been the year before. Sophie told us she made the snowmen for a little boy who loved going outside in snowstorms to make snowman families. She insisted we take some with us. My wife later commented that she felt Sophie kept a deeper story to herself."

"What do you mean?" Ben asked, knowing the answer.

"With a degree in counseling, my wife wrote about family issues before retiring. She sensed Sophie was saying so much more with the words she chose."

Ben thanked Lawrence for the information. He told him he'd be in touch. He couldn't get off the phone fast enough for once he did he started to cry. He couldn't stop. Ben cried so hard that he was gasping for air. The little boy who'd sat alone in the back of a sleigh, on a journey to meet his mommy and daddy was crying for that other mother he'd known as Sophie—the young woman who'd bundle him up and take him out behind the orphanage to make snowmen in the fields. Ben remembered how they'd stay outside and roll snowballs even in the worst of weather. Together they'd lift smaller snowballs on top of large ones.

That little boy was certain he did most of the lifting. After all, Sophie told him he did. They'd gather sticks for arms and coal or stones for the eyes and mouths. Sophie would save carrots from the kitchen for noses and stay up late knitting mittens, scarves, and hats. It was something seeing those snowmen in the fields. They'd make baby snowmen, brother and sister snowmen, mommy snowmen, and daddy snowmen. They'd give them names. They'd pretend what the families were doing and saying. They'd laugh and play in the snow. When they went back inside, they'd have hot chocolate as they looked out the window at all the families together. Despite the storm all around them, the families stayed together.

Ben could feel the stinging of his frozen feet and fingers as he remembered rolling snowball after snowball and laughing and playing so hard with Sophie that stinging feet and fingers didn't matter. Minutes passed before Ben was able to explain.

"It all makes sense now, Ellie. Lawrence said Sophie explained the snowmen are for a little boy she once knew who liked to go outside in snowstorms and make snowmen families. That little boy is me, Ellie. I remember how we'd stay outside for the longest time and make families out of the snow. Some families had two kids; some had three, and some had grandparents."

Ben stopped as he remembered another time out in the snow in those rambling fields that seemed to go way beyond the orphanage. But then he was little and the world was big. "There were only two snowmen—a mother and a little boy. Sophie explained how different families can be. She told me that what mattered was that they loved each other, but she was crying. That was the last snowman family we made."

"What a beautiful way for her to tell you she loved you, Ben. All these years she's been sending you her love. Something tells me that's what you couldn't put your finger on. You felt it but you didn't have the details—and now you do."

"And now I'm going to search for her, Ellie. Even though I'm afraid of what I might discover, I have to go find out."

The rest of the day was spent completing last minute touches throughout the stone home about to welcome Christmas. That's what was done every year in late December. But this year it turned out the anticipation was even greater as plans were made for a trip to Portsmouth in the morning. Ellie would take care of things at home, including answering Henry's questions as to where Ben and Andy were should he come around.

It was close to midnight by the time Ellie got around to opening the box sitting on the dining room table. It was one of those things where she needed time to think about it before doing it. She had to be ready for whatever she might find. Ever since losing Abbey to cancer, Ellie realized how close they'd been; how much Abbey meant to her.

Digging into the Styrofoam packing, she felt a box with a ribbon around it. Pulling it out, she stopped to read the tag. Ellie recognized Steve's handwriting simply stating, *To Ellie and family—with love, Greta.* Standing by the table with the wind singing its song, Ellie remembered watching Ben as he held his mother's letter. Now it was her turn to open something sealed with love. Those are the gifts that remain a gift forever. Not even trying to stop the tears, Ellie pulled the ribbon off and opened the box decorated with snowmen. *Of course there'd be snowmen,* she thought. *This is the Christmas for snowmen.*

Underneath layers of more packing, Ellie found a gift wrapped in newsprint covered with little red and green handprints. Most were smudged. Some were minus a finger or two but she could tell whoever orchestrated the project had used poster paints. She knew they were Greta's handprints—the granddaughter Abbey never knew. *These handprints are just what Abbey would have done. I'm sure Abbey is smiling.* It took a few more minutes before Ellie opened the gift and when she did, she had to sit down. It was a photo of Abbey's family. *Abbey left her mark,* Ellie thought, looking at the beautiful family in front of her. Greta was sitting on her grandfather's lap. *She looks like Abbey. She's even holding onto a book. Abbey would have loved that.* Ellie noted the tree in the background, decorated with the same ornaments Abbey brought out every year. Her boys looked well. They looked happy, and that's all a mother ever wants for her children. Looking closer, Ellie noted Meg was expecting. *How nice, Greta will be a big sister. Abbey and Steve will have another grandchild.*

Ellie had been so focused on the picture that at first, she hadn't noticed an envelope taped to the back of the frame. It was addressed to, *Ellie, Ben, and family.* As she started to open the envelope, Ellie's thoughts went back to that particular winter night down on the creek when two young cousins were discussing life with Christmas a heartbeat away. While they had other cousins, Ellie and Abbey were inseparable.

"We'll always be together on Christmas, Ellie."

"We will, Abbey. Best cousins are always together—even when they aren't."

"If we aren't, all you have to do is look up at the moon. I'll be looking at the moon, too—the very same moon looking down on us right now."

"And when we look up at the moon, we'll be saying Merry Christmas to each other, Abbey."

"Yes we will, Ellie."

It was quiet on the ice for a minute as two cousins looked up towards the heavens.

"Merry Christmas, Ellie."

"Merry Christmas, Abbey."

In the busy world of adulthood, we tend to forget little smidgens of times tucked away somewhere inside us. When we bother to find them, the moment is breathtaking. Walking into the front room, Ellie looked up at the moon. It was as full and wondrous as that night of long ago down at the creek. As she stood there, stars circling the moon seemed to shimmer all the more. She knew it was Abbey. In her heart, she knew her cousin was saying Merry Christmas. *Merry Christmas, Abbey—my most favorite cousin of all—Merry Christmas.*

A few minutes later, Ellie was reading a card from the love of Abbey's life.

Ellie,

I hope this note finds you well. I thought you'd enjoy this latest photo. You'll see Abbey's spirit lives on through Greta.

The boys say hello. Eric's move from Wall Street to chef was a good one. His restaurant, opened this past August, continues to receive 5-star reviews. He and Meg will welcome their second child in May. It's a boy, Ellie. Abbey will have a grandson.

Sammy surprised us by proposing to Cate while filming in Brazil. The wedding will take place here at the farmhouse next Christmas. It would mean so much to all of us if you and your family could join us. I'll keep you informed as we go along. I wish you a Merry Christmas, Ellie.

My love to all,

Steve

With the photo sitting in the front room where the moon came shining through, Ellie looked out the window one more time. Then, turning out the lights, Ellie went upstairs, her focus returning to a woman named Sophie.

Chapter Twenty-Three

THE MAIN ROADS WERE CLEAR ALL the way to the state line and into New Hampshire. Ben followed Lawrence's directions straight to downtown Portsmouth. If ever there was a perfect image of the holidays, it was this place on the sea coast. Historic buildings mingled with blocks of retailers. Little shops with windows dressed for the season were scattered among upscale boutiques and restaurants for any taste or budget.

"Are you hungry?"

"That's up to you," said Andy. "What's the plan?"

"I told your mother we'd be back sometime tonight."

"Then let's go find her, Dad."

After parking the truck, Ben and Andy stepped out onto Market Square bustling with shoppers this last weekend before Christmas. There were so many quaint shops, all with that homespun New England feel. Although he'd been told how to find the shop, Ben didn't need any help. He saw the sign up on the left. Crossing the street, they hurried to the small-paned window showing bolts of fabric and a little black Singer sewing machine. It was just as Ben had imagined. Over the doorway was a canopy. You had to walk down two cobblestone steps to get to the old, wooden Dutch door. It was the sort of door Ben would have chosen. It fit the frame of the building. It worked within the theme of Market

Street. He realized his flair for putting things together didn't come out of the blue. It had roots.

Peeking through one of the windows, Andy could see a small light on towards the back. A partially pulled curtain in an archway blocked his ability to see more.

"There's no sign saying the place is closed or that she's sick. Let's go in, Dad."

Even before Andy finished talking, Ben had his hand on the brass doorknob. He tried turning it, but it wouldn't budge. The door was locked.

"Now what do we do?" asked Andy.

"Let's ask around. Obviously someone's been here at some point."

While people in neighboring businesses told them they'd seen someone coming in and out in recent weeks, they couldn't verify that it was Sophie.

A silversmith next door explained, "Sophie's been sick. But lately I've noticed the closed sign's been down. I've seen customers coming in and out, but I can't say if Sophie's been the one inside."

"So whoever comes and goes does so randomly?" asked Ben.

"I don't keep watch. I can only say the place isn't open on a regular basis."

"Have you seen anyone today?"

Andy answered the question. "There weren't any footprints in the snow on the steps but ours, Dad."

Thanking the artisan, Ben decided they would grab a late lunch. He'd noticed a place right across the street. They'd be able to keep watch while eating.

Both he and Andy were hungrier than they realized. They stayed longer than planned. When Ben went up to pay the bill, Andy came rushing to get him.

"I saw her, Dad. I saw your mother! I know it's your mother! She's there! Right now, she's there! Hurry!"

Ben was all thumbs. He left one heck of a tip before they flew out the door.

Chapter Twenty-Four

WITH THE TRAFFIC, IT SEEMED LIKE it took forever to cross the street. Catching up to his father, Andy asked, "Want me to go first, Dad?"

Ben didn't reply. He was down the front steps with his hand on the doorknob. This time when he turned it, the door opened, and as it did, a little bell above it tinkled. She wasn't in sight. After Andy was inside, Ben shut the door, and the little bell tinkled again, but still no Sophie. Ben did hear music. It was turned down low, but he recognized Perry Como singing "White Christmas." He'd heard it before when he was little.

Looking around, Ben noticed the tree in the window covered with little snowmen. The scent of fabric and yarn mingling with old wood and tapestries added to the character of the intriguing little shop. A front counter held a cash register that must have been an original—no computer here. Sitting next to the cash register were order pads, the kind waitresses use. Mahogany shelves appeared worn, probably by bolts of fabric sitting on them over the years. There was so much fabric. Primitive cupboards held woolens and corduroys, linens and cottons. Velvets and organzas, taffetas and brocades were off on their own, taking up an entire wall. An oak pedestal table was in the center of the room. With scissors and yardsticks sitting on top, it was obvious the table was where Sophie cut the fabric. Sitting next to that archway somewhat covered by a curtain was a dry sink holding buttons, zippers, and decorative items. Wainscoting halfway up the walls surrounded the room. A shelf holding plants, small crocks, and tin boxes sat above the front window.

It was an orange cat jumping up on the table that aroused someone's attention in a back room. "I heard you jump up there, old girl. Get down. You know I don't like you on the table."

The cat reacted, darting off the table and running under the curtain. Again that someone spoke. "I'm pinning fabric. I'll be out in a minute."

Ben couldn't wait. He hesitated, realizing once he pulled the curtain back, his world would change. Andy whispered to his father to go, so that's what Ben did.

To his surprise, he walked into a small room with a rambling desk full of compartments stuffed with papers, swatches, stray buttons, and zippers. Legal pads with sketches of dresses, pants, and gowns were everywhere. A calendar from two years back was still hanging on the wall, but it didn't matter. The calendar featured Norman Rockwell art. It fit the mood. A small picture in a black frame sitting on a shelf above the desk caught Ben's attention. He couldn't help it. His reaction was spontaneous. He reached for the picture, and as he did, the cat jumped up, startling him. He held onto the frame, but papers fell to the floor. Ben didn't notice any of that. He was staring at a photo of a young mother with her little boy. It was the same photo he'd found at the summer camp.

"You silly cat. I know what you did. Get down off the—"

The old woman was surprised to find someone standing at her desk. Adjusting glasses sitting at the tip of her nose, she asked, "Can I help you, young man?"

Ben couldn't speak. He couldn't look up. He stood there.

"Do you need some material cut?" Sophie asked, getting a little closer to Ben.

That's when she noticed what he was holding. She saw tears streaming down his cheeks. A clock ticking on the marble mantel of an old fireplace announced a new hour. It also gave Ben the nerve to speak.

"I remember," he said and then stopped, wiping away the tears. "I remember that clock. When it rang out 5 PM, we'd file into the dining room, one by one. But sometimes ..." Ben hesitated, his voice cracking, tears falling as he looked at Sophie. "Sometimes I'd wait to go in . . . with you."

Not even the cat purring, or the clock ticking, or the muffled grunts and groans from passersby were heard by the two in that little room with the crowded desk. Except for a gasp, Sophie stood in silence, reaching for the back of a chair to steady herself despite the use of a cane. She stared at the young man in front of her, who stared back. She was shorter than he'd imagined, with a tape measure draped around her neck over a single strand of pearls. Her gray hair was gathered up in a bun, kept in place with hair combs. It all added to her character. Stray wisps of hair fell down upon her forehead above her soft brown eyes. Though her face was wrinkled by years passing by, her high cheekbones and natural hue offered her a unique sort of beauty. Wrapped in a camel-colored cardigan with pockets bulging over a basic wool dress, her simplicity was apparent. So was her strength when she found the words.

"Sometimes you'd finish your dinner before me, and when you did, my little boy, you'd help me finish mine. My sweet Benny. My dear little boy! You've grown into such a handsome man. I have missed you, my son, every second of every day. God has answered my prayers, my Benny. God has brought you home."

Despite her shortness and the fact that she walked with a limp, Sophie was able to reach up and cradle Ben's face in her hands. Nothing could have stopped her. He was her child. She kept outlining his face with her fingers as she looked into his eyes. Pulling him near, she kissed his forehead again and again.

"My Benny. My sweet, sweet Benny. I've prayed that you were safe, that you were happy. I've hoped and prayed for this moment. I've imagined it over and over in my mind. I love you, my son."

Sophie could no longer hold back the tears as she hugged her child. The spirit of the season took on an even deeper meaning inside the little shop on Market Street.

Chapter Twenty-Five

Though it seemed as if the world had gone away, reality set in when the little bell above the front door announced a customer. Actually, there were two. One was picking up a special order. The other, an older gentleman, was shopping for his wife.

"I've bought the jewelry, and the clothing, and the tickets to Hawaii. I was hoping to find something not in every boutique or online site. I'm in need of something that I can't put my finger on."

Distracted by Ben and curious about Andy, Sophie tried staying attentive to the rather tall man dressed in a tailored suit and an overcoat. She could tell he'd paid top dollar for both.

"I'm a fabric shop, sir. Does your wife sew?"

"Not in years."

"Think she'd be interested in getting back to it?"

"She used to sew all the time. She said it was relaxing. But that was before the accident."

Sophie didn't feel it was her place to question this stranger. It turned out she didn't have to.

"When we lost our son, she lost interest in everything. For some reason I thought of your shop today. I go by here all the time."

Sophie put herself in the woman's place. It was easy to do. She'd experienced the same pain and wondering, right up to a few minutes ago.

Only another mother could understand. That's when Sophie knew what this man was searching for.

"These snowmen were made by a mother who lost her little boy. They'd have fun playing in the snow, making snowmen—all kinds of snowman families, they called them. When they'd go back inside, the mother would make them hot chocolate. Then they'd sit together by a big window and make up stories about the snowmen outside. These little snowmen helped her. They might do the same for your wife."

To hear this story straight from his mother was a powerful thing. Ben held back more tears as the man asked Sophie a question.

"May I ask how that mother is doing today?"

"I'm doing fine, sir. I'm doing gloriously fine."

Moving to the register, Sophie wrote something on a slip of paper. Then she went to the Christmas tree and picked out half a dozen or so of the snowmen. Laying them on the oak table, she wrapped each one in tissue paper. Then she placed them inside a brown bag with a handle.

"Give these to your wife, sir. Tell her the story behind them."

Sophie handed him the bag along with that slip of paper. "Believe it or not, I have a cell phone. This is the number. If she ever feels like she needs someone to talk to who's been in her shoes, I am here for her. And you, sir—I am here for you, too. I recognize the pain in your eyes."

"I knew the answer was here," the man said, as tears fell. "I didn't know what it was, but I knew I'd find it. I miss my wife. I feel as if I've lost her forever."

"Her sorrow runs deep. A mother carries a child in her womb for nine months. Then she has to share that child with the world, and when the world is cruel, the pain is excruciating. But I am here to say there is a plan. You have not lost your wife forever. This is the season of hope. Take these snowmen as my gift to the both of you ... and a very merry Christmas, sir."

"I want to pay you."

"You've paid me in many ways."

"May I ask your name?"

"Sophie. My name is Sophie."

"Thank you, Sophie. A very merry Christmas to you and your family."

Once the gentleman was out of sight, Sophie locked the door and pulled the curtain.

"When I look at you, Benny, I see a man secure in himself; content where life has taken him, and that, my Benny, warms my heart."

Moving to Andy's side, she continued. "I see my father's eyes in this young man."

"This is my son, Andy. He couldn't wait to meet his grandmother."

"I felt I was a grandmother. I couldn't wait to meet you, Andy."

"You're exactly as I imagined."

"Short, with a cane?" Sophie laughed.

"A survivor—like my dad."

"Oh, Benny, he's breaking my heart. Give your grandmother a hug, Andy."

It ended up being the three of them sharing an embrace as Ben told Sophie about Maggie.

"I have a granddaughter in Europe! Such spunk! You two should have warned me you were coming. I'm out of tissues!"

Wiping away tears with the sleeve of her sweater, Sophie added, "Come back to my workroom. We can sit and talk over a cup of tea. Do you drink tea, Andy?"

"My mom got me used to it."

"I want to hear about your mom. I want to hear about all of you. This truly is a Christmas miracle!"

Chapter Twenty-Six

It could have been because the work area was so small that the conversation seemed so intense if it weren't for the fact they were family members making up for years apart. Even though they were squeezed in among bolts of cottons and linens, and odds and ends of buttons, hooks, and eyes were everywhere on the small table, they were lucky. Sometimes families don't get to make up for years apart for one reason or another. Some allow the passing of time as an excuse not to try.

"Take these teacups, Benny. They belonged to your great-grandmother. Now I can hand them down as was the intention when they were given to me."

"I was told your parents died when you were young."

"Sadly that's true. Thankfully the nuns welcomed me with open arms. Years later, I contacted what relatives I could find. They weren't too interested in an adult orphan with polio so they appeased me with a few heirlooms. That was fine with me. I wasn't used to a family like that. My family had been the orphanage."

"That's probably why Bobby has so many orphans in his database. They want to stay connected."

It took Ben a good fifteen minutes to explain Bobby and his database.

"I remember Bobby standing at the kitchen door with a string of fish and a big smile. I could have cooked his catch any old way, and he would have been happy."

Next Ben explained about meeting Paul's family and learning about letters written to him over the years, including Sophie's.

"Paul took so many under his wing. I'll forever be grateful to his family for sharing those letters with you."

Another cup of tea and they were still talking as fast as they could. Sophie was amazed that they lived less than four hours away and that Ben had gone in search of Sister Mary Beth and found her. She wasn't surprised that her boy, who'd loved building with Lincoln Logs, had grown up to be an architect, or that both he and Andy loved the guitar.

"My father played the guitar until he met my mother," Sophie recalled. "Love can change your life in unexpected ways. You're never the same."

Ben noticed a shift in tone. He felt as if he'd known her all his life, even down to little idiosyncrasies like that mellowed voice when she spoke of falling in love. She didn't say if she'd ever married. He left it alone for now.

"Looks like you've made a good life for yourself here," said Ben.

"I stumbled upon this area years back. With independent fabric stores becoming harder to find, I feel my location has proven invaluable. Of course good eyesight helps. I can still thread a needle!"

"Do you live upstairs, Grandma?"

"No. I hold sewing classes up there. Believe it or not, some people still want to learn how to sew, even young people. Others want to get back into it."

"Do you live far from here?"

"I have a small stone home down by the water, Andy. I can walk back and forth. Best part about that is I have a sewing room with a tremendous view."

"That's amazing. We live in an old stone home," remarked Ben. "Do you remember Henry? He told me how you enjoyed going horseback riding with him. He has a stone home not far from ours."

Fussing with her hair, Sophie appeared to be figuring something out before replying. "I do. I do remember Henry. Is he ... well?"

"He seems to be doing okay. I think he misses Helen more than he lets on."

"I remember he'd married."

"Helen passed away some years back. But I keep him busy. He works harder than most half his age."

"I'm not surprised," Sophie started to say something, but she paused before continuing. "Henry comes from a hardworking family."

"He took us by sleigh down to the summer camp."

"You know about the camp, Benny? Why did you go there?"

"I was searching for clues—any clues—as to how I might find you. Henry told us about the camp."

"Are the buildings still there?"

"Yes. They're in pretty good shape, considering they've been neglected."

"The decision to close the camp was sudden," she said. "I only had enough time to box everything up. That camp holds so many wonderful memories. Did you remember anything being down there?"

"Some things came in bits and pieces."

"You were so young."

"What hit me first was the creaking sound of the oven door. I remembered lying in my bed hearing you in the kitchen. I also remembered an old cupboard by the back door."

"Do you remember rolling out cookie dough and cutting out shapes for tarts?"

"They were the best!"

"I'm still making them," replied Sophie. "Every time I do, I picture you covered in flour. You were so serious. You wanted every shape to be perfect. It must have been that builder in you!"

Getting up from the table, Sophie fussed about the cupboards and came back with a plate full of tarts. "They taste better warm."

"They still smell the same! You have to try one, Andy."

One tart led to another as the conversation turned to something Ben pulled out of his coat pocket. He'd found it at the summer camp.

"I keep this letter with me. I was afraid the letter and this picture would be all I'd ever have of you."

Sophie couldn't help it. The tears were streaming down her face even before holding the letter. It was quiet in the fabric shop despite the frenzy out along the sidewalks. After reading the letter, Sophie put down her glasses.

"I didn't know what to do, Benny. I never thought I'd see you again. This letter was my way of expressing to you what I felt at what remains the saddest time in my life. I couldn't give you what every child should have—a stable home. I handed you over to God and kept you in my heart. Every time I'd see a little boy, I'd think maybe that was you, especially if he had freckles, as you did, or smiled a certain way. When it was your birthday, I'd sing to you. On Christmas I imagined you leaving cookies for Santa, hanging your stocking, and, in the morning, flying down stairs. I wondered how you were doing in school, wondered if you disliked science as I did. I was frightened you might be sick, and if you were, I felt guilty I wasn't there. I imagined you all grown up. I worried you might have gone off to war. I was curious if you'd fallen in love, and if you had, what her name was and if you were happy." Sophie stopped to take a breath, but just for a moment.

"Life has a way of taking us down our path without us even knowing it. Now here you are a grown man, sitting with me at this table, bringing me the letter I wrote to you when life was separating us."

Ben felt like a little boy, not the well-known architect sought out by so many. He kissed his mother's hands, wiped away her tears. "Now that I've found you, I'll never let you go. I understand the sacrifices you made for me. Henry told me of your strength."

"Henry's the strongest and yet most gentle man I've ever known."

"His kindness is what's struck me, especially on Christmas Eve."

"I don't understand, Benny."

"Henry and Helen never had a family, so on Christmas Eve they'd open their home to less fortunate children. Dressed as Santa Claus, Henry would take the kids for sleigh rides. Later Helen served them cookies and hot chocolate."

"It sounds as if they were happy."

"I think so, although at times I feel there is something Henry's holding back."

"He didn't hold back on Christmas Eve!"

"No, he didn't, Andy. He and Helen welcomed so many into their home." Ben hesitated, but only for a moment. "I'd like you to come to our home for Christmas, Mom."

"Oh, Benny! I couldn't! I have my cat, and my shop, and the lessons ... my home, oh I couldn't...I don't know! Christmas Eve is tomorrow, Benny."

"Andy and I will wait for you. Whatever you have to do, we'll wait for you."

"I don't know," Sophie repeated, getting up for more tarts.

She stayed there, looking out a window while snipping some dry leaves off a Christmas cactus. Fussing with her hair combs, Sophie smoothed out her sweater. Then she turned back around. "I think you should head back soon, while the weather holds."

"But I told you we'll wait for you."

"I'm an old lady, Benny. I have to get my thoughts together. I'm in shock that you are here."

"I can't leave you. I just found you."

Taking Benny's hands in hers, Sophie replied, "I will come tomorrow on the train, if you are able to pick me up ... if it isn't an inconvenience to you and your family."

"You *are* my family, Mom. I'll pick you up anytime, anywhere."

It took Ben a good hour to make the travel arrangements. He was lucky to get her a seat with Christmas Eve less than twenty-four hours away. After buying the ticket and coordinating taxi service to the station, Ben went next door to the silversmith's and asked if he'd keep an eye on the shop while she was away. As for the orange cat, Sophie told him that a young girl who'd taken sewing lessons would be happy to care for her.

"But I don't have any gifts, Benny. I want to bring something special to Ellie."

"Wherever you want to go shopping, we'll take you."

Sophie hurried into the shop.

Pulling back a curtain hiding a small storage space, Sophie moved things around until she found an old hatbox.

"A hat, Grandma?"

"Wait and see, Andy." Removing the top, Sophie reached inside. Pushing through remnants cut in all sizes and shapes, she pulled out a piece of cotton wrapped around something small. Placing it on the counter, she explained. "This was the first little snowman made, and it was made by you, Benny. Or at least you helped."

"I helped?"

"We'd been outside in a snowstorm making snowmen. When we got back inside, you wanted to make another one so I pulled out my sewing basket, and this is what we created. You picked out the fabric. You painted the eyes." Sophie smiled. "And you signed it."

Turning it upside down, Sophie showed Ben a small, squiggled letter B.

"Once the orphanage closed and you'd been placed, I had to keep making the snowmen. It was my way of keeping in touch with you. Whenever I met or heard of others who'd lived with us, I gave or sent them snowmen. I felt they were part of our family. They'd each earned a snowman family of their own."

Wrapping the snowman up in the piece of cotton, Sophie put it back in the hatbox.

"Ellie will love your gift, Mom. She fell in love with the snowmen you left with me. She sensed how special they were before knowing anything about them."

"Your Ellie sounds like a lovely woman, Benny."

After taking Sophie where she had to go in order to be ready for the next day, Ben brought her back to the fabric shop. Sophie explained she still had a special order to finish.

"A man, probably a little younger than you, Benny, came in last week. He'd heard about the snowmen. He told me his wife's father had died earlier in the year and he was hoping I'd have time to make four identical snowmen. They had to have glasses painted on their faces. He brought me a flannel shirt worn by his father-in-law and asked that each be dressed in a coat made from the shirt. I have two more to go."

"You're like Henry, Mom. You give the true meaning of Christmas to others at a time when that's the gift they need."

"I'm an old lady who has to keep her fingers busy. The pleasure I get from sewing is immeasurable."

"Taking a project from the drawing board to finish gives me that rush."

"I get it with the guitar," added Andy.

"You both inherited the creative gene," joked Sophie, who insisted they get back on the road.

Ben understood. She needed her space. He'd walked into her world unannounced, and before she walked into his, she needed to get her thoughts together. Ben was the same way. That was why he'd converted the carriage house into his workspace. It was more therapeutic than anything.

Writing down his cell number, Ben asked her to call him with any concerns she might have about anything. He realized she took great pride in being independent. He only wanted to be there, after years of being apart.

"I'll be waiting for you at the station."

"I'll be there, my boy. I'll be there."

"By the way," he added, opening the door with the little bell tinkling. "I never liked science."

After sharing a good laugh, Sophie asked them to wait a second. She was back in seconds, handing Andy some tarts sealed in a plastic bag. "I bet you drive the girls crazy, playing that guitar of yours. Probably like your father did!"

LATER, RIDING THROUGH A LIGHT SNOWFALL, Andy admitted that it was hard leaving Sophie. "She's pretty cool, Dad. Grandma reminds me of you."

"How so?"

"When we were sitting at the table, I looked around. Little things tell her story, as little things tell yours. Now I understand. Life isn't the big stuff."

Ben kept driving as he realized his son had grown up—right there—right beside him as they headed home. Ben felt like yelling from the mountain tops. *He's going to make it out there. He's going to be okay.*

Sometimes when you're a parent you wonder if your child gets it. You try to set examples, as one day blends into another. You try while overcoming hurdles, solving problems, providing, worrying, and wondering if anything at all has sunk in, especially when they reach that age when nothing seems as if it has and nothing ever will.

"Tell me again about Hendrix, Dad."

And so it went. As two guitarists talked about their craft while driving along the interstate and as an old woman's fingers were kept busy dressing little snowmen in a fabric shop by the seacoast, thoughts of a family reunited filled their very happy hearts. We never know what a day may bring.

Chapter Twenty-Seven

Ben called Ellie after Andy fell asleep plugged into his music. They talked right up until he pulled onto their road, and they stayed up talking past 2 AM. Ellie told Ben that Henry had stacked the wood and made a few trips to town for her.

"I didn't let on where you'd gone. When he left, he wasn't sure if he'd make it tomorrow for dinner."

"I'd tell him Sophie was coming, but I'd like to surprise him."

When morning broke, they were back at it again. Ben spent a long time on the phone with Bobby.

"Give Sophie my best. I'm happy for the both of you. I'll get the word out about your spending Christmas together."

Despite the fact there'd only be a few gathered this night, Ellie didn't hold back. She placed the heirloom china on the embroidered tablecloth that had been handed down through generations in Ellie's family. After the holidays, she would take it to the cleaners. Then she'd put it back in the cedar chest in the spare bedroom where Sophie would be sleeping.

"That room, with its bookcases and window with a great view, was made for her, Ellie. I hope there's a full moon. What a sight that would be!"

"I remember when Maggie would stand in front of that window

on Christmas Eve, waiting, certain she'd be able to reach out and touch Santa's sleigh."

"That reminds me of Christmas mornings at the orphanage. After we'd finish eating pancakes, we'd hear bells ringing. That meant Santa and his elf were coming. We'd keep singing while Santa called us up one by one. He'd give each of us two presents and a stocking with an orange and socks and a few other things. I don't remember much more, except being excited that Santa knew my name. He told me I was a good boy."

"Do you remember Sophie being there with you?

"No, but yesterday she told me she was the elf!"

Andy interrupted them as he came through the back door. He explained he'd been at Henry's. He'd convinced him to come for dinner later.

"Great! How did you do that?"

"He was telling me some of his Christmas Eve stories, Dad. All I said was Helen would be happy if she knew he'd be taking the sleigh out on Christmas Eve."

With Sophie coming, they all were happy that Henry would be joining them.

After Ellie fixed a late lunch, Ben decided he'd better get on the road.

"I want to give myself plenty of time. If all goes well, I should be back no later than six o'clock."

Standing in the front window, Ellie watched as Ben drove out of sight. Thoughts of him as a little boy at Christmastime in the orphanage brought tears to her eyes.

Life has a way of making sense of it all, she thought. *Despite obstacles, that little boy has grown into a fine and decent man.*

Now that fine and decent man was on a new path. Sometimes when we think we know what lies ahead, our path takes an unmarked turn.

Chapter Twenty-Eight

THERE WAS SOMETHING HOLLYWOOD—LIKE BEING IN the old station on Christmas Eve. The weathered mahogany and cobblestone walkway provided a perfect backdrop for a Christmas classic. Surely Fonda or Hepburn must have played a role in such a scene once upon a time. Little shops were built around a towering clock which chimed on the half hour. A newsstand void of any hint of computers and wireless sprawled out against a brick wall in a far corner. The smell of newsprint mixed with cigars and chewing tobacco reminded Ben of going with his adoptive father for papers every Sunday morning. In contrast, an Internet café was nearby.

The station was bustling with travelers. Most were carrying gifts. Most looked excited to get to where they were headed. Checking the train arrivals, Ben noted Sophie's was on time. With a good hour yet to go, he bought a coffee and a paper and sat down where he'd be able to keep track of the arrivals. Having been caught up in a whirlwind, this was the first time he'd had to think about the last twenty-four hours. If he didn't know any better, he would have thought it all had been a dream or one of those Hollywood-like scripts.

Ben became curious about the families rushing by. They came in all sizes and ages, and from all walks of life. He wondered how many were happy. He wondered if any of the people had been adopted. A little while later, heeding the announcement over the loudspeaker of a certain train's arrival, he was off to meet his mother.

Being a seasoned commuter, Ben knew she'd probably be one of the last ones off the train. But the longer he stood waiting, the more anxious he became. What if she'd changed her mind? What if yesterday had been too much for her? Ben had himself in such a tizzy that he didn't hear his name being called. However, he did see a hand waving, holding an oversized hatbox wrapped in a big red bow.

"Benny! I'm over here, Benny!"

He heard her now. "I'm coming, Mom! I'm coming!"

Pushing through the crowd, flashbacks to what must have been the last time he'd seen her, before yesterday, came at him like the people darting in and out all around him.

He could hear bells ringing. Ben figured they must have been on horses hitched to a certain sleigh decorated in pine boughs. He saw a beautiful young woman holding onto a blanket as someone lifted him into the sleigh. Ben knew it was Henry. He knew it was Christmas Eve. He knew the nun sitting in the sleigh was Sister Mary Beth. She handed him his teddy bear and covered him up. There were two other children sitting next to him. Sister Mary Beth covered them up too after pushing a cardboard box Henry had handed her under the seat. As the sleigh headed into the night, Ben turned around and saw that young woman crying and waving frantically, just like Sophie now waving in the midst of a crowd. This time Ben wouldn't lose her.

Searching the mass of people, he spotted her again, still waving, with silver bracelets dangling over the tops of long red gloves. She fit right into his movie theme, wearing a wide-brimmed felt-like hat with what looked like feathers sticking out along the side and a long wool coat with a fur collar.

"Stay there, Mom. I'm coming! I'm coming, Mom!"

And he did. Pulling Sophie close, Ben protected her from the crush of others in a hurry. Taking her bag and the hatbox in one hand and wrapping his other arm around her, Ben led her to the side of the track.

"Are you okay, Mom?"

"Now that my knight in shining armor has saved me, I am."

"Were you able to get everything off the train?"

"I'm thrifty, Benny. I also travel light."

"We'll wait for the area to clear. Then I'll get you upstairs and situated before I get the car. Let's go home, Mom."

"Whatever you say, Benny."

It all went like clockwork. Ben had Sophie out of the terminal without a hitch. He didn't mention a thing about Henry joining them for dinner. After all, Christmas is about surprises—no matter how old you are.

Chapter Twenty-Nine

It was pitch dark out as they left the station. You'd never know it though, with the landscape glowing in twinkling lights wrapped around houses, trees, and fences all under glistening stars and a moon made for romantics and Christmas believers. Turning onto the road leading home, Ben again told Sophie how happy he was to have her home for Christmas.

"I have a dear friend with whom I've spent the holiday ever since her husband passed away. It has to be over ten years now, and every year that we've been together, she's asked me if I have any family. It wasn't until recently that I told her about my parents dying and my growing up in the orphanage. I never told her I had a son." Sophie paused. "Yesterday I called her to say I wouldn't be doing the cooking this year because I was spending Christmas with my son and his family."

"What was her reaction?"

"She wasn't surprised. She told me she'd sensed there was something I wasn't sharing. I'm convinced when one's heart aches, others can hear it."

"Ellie saw sadness in my eyes even before I told her of the adoption."

"That shows how well she knows you, Benny. Other women might have felt threatened."

"I pulled away from her ... from everyone, for a time. I had to absorb the news. We'd never held anything back so it was hard for Ellie seeing me struggle and keeping her at a distance. Since I blurted it out, she's been my rock which is what she's been from the beginning. She is my best friend."

"I'm happy for you, Benny. What you and Ellie have takes work. So often what brings people together gets lost over the years. I hear this sort of chatter when giving my lessons."

"What do you tell them?"

"I'm afraid I am no expert on marriage."

Benny wanted to take that subject a little further, but even though she was his mother, he felt they needed more time together before getting into those details.

"I'm sorry my actions caused you pain, Benny."

"If anything, it's made me stronger. It's reminded me how fortunate I am to have Ellie by my side. Now that I've found you, I feel whole. I never did before." Going around a sharp curve, Ben told Sophie they were almost home.

"That sounds marvelous, Benny. I've missed you."

"I've missed you, even when I didn't realize it was you I was missing."

"It's starting to snow. For a long time I couldn't stand to watch it snow. It made me cry. Then one November night I found myself walking home in a snowstorm, and the more I walked, the more I loved being surrounded by snowflakes again. Instead of being sad, I chose to celebrate the snow. We do have choices in life. Some choices, like embracing a snowfall, may seem simple, but to me it was being able to look back and remember my little boy out in the snow without becoming overwhelmed by sadness and guilt. I accepted the fact that I'd done the best I could at that particular moment."

"Maggie and Andy continue to remind me about making choices in life. I can't say I agree with some they've made, but I support them."

"They're spreading their wings. They can't stay in the nest forever."

"We'll call Maggie in the morning. Hard to believe she won't be here on Christmas morning."

"I hear a father missing a daughter."

"When she was little, Maggie would come in early Christmas morning and wake me to go downstairs with her to see if Santa had come. Once she was assured that he'd been there, I'd carry her back upstairs and tuck her into bed. She'd go right to sleep after I promised not to tell her mother. It was our little secret."

"Little secrets like that strengthen a bond. They take on a meaning all their own."

"Just like rolling snowballs in a blizzard."

"Just like it, Benny."

As they pulled into a driveway defined by pine and poplar trees and cedar hedges, Sophie gazed at Ben's house. Candles were lighting every window, and a tree standing near the front door was sparkling with silver tinsel.

"Your home is beautifully decorated, Benny. It belongs in a magazine."

"Every year I add a bit more detail, while making sure I don't overdo it. That's when I feel it all gets lost."

Even before Ben turned the car off, Andy was down the front steps.

"Grandma! Hi! We've been waiting for you."

While Sophie collected her things, Andy whispered to his father that Henry had called to say he was going to be late. "He told Mom we could start without him."

"There's nothing more we can do, Andy."

"Are you two talking about me again?"

"Yes we are, Mom. You'd better get used to it!"

When Ben opened the front door, Ellie was there to greet Sophie. Neither one could hold back the tears.

While Andy took Sophie's stuff up to her room, Ben put the car away. When they got back to the kitchen, Ellie and Sophie were talking like long-lost friends.

"Your mom is amazing, honey."

"Well, she *is* my mother!"

"And I am so happy to be here," said Sophie.

"Our home is your home."

"Thank you, Benny. Thank you."

"Would you like a glass of wine or eggnog?"

"A glass of wine would hit the spot!"

"I bought some Pinot Noir," Ellie said. "I was told it compliments turkey."

"That it does, Ellie," added Sophie.

"Ben, why don't you take Sophie into the front room? Andy, could you put this tray of hors d'oeuvres on the coffee table? I'll be right in with the wine. Would you like some eggnog, Ben?"

"Yes. Thanks honey."

Aromas from the kitchen mingling with those of the tree only added to the moment. Ben stoked the fire as the snow kept falling.

"I remember sewing those snowmen for you, Benny. I was frantic that something of me stayed with you."

"As a mother, I can't imagine how you felt," spoke Ellie after handing Sophie her glass of wine. "It was an unselfish act on your part."

"It was a different time, Ellie. Unwed mothers were tarred and feathered and sent off in secrecy to give birth, and then they returned as if nothing had occurred. They couldn't share how their labor had been; something mothers like to do. They couldn't give an account of how the delivery went or how absolutely breathtaking their babies were, because in the eyes of others, there was no baby, so therefore there had been no grueling labor or exhausting delivery."

"That's pretty crude," said Andy. "Why does any of that matter?"

"It doesn't, Andy," Ben remarked. "Sadly, it once did."

"I'm a firm believer that there's a reason for everything. That's where your faith comes in," added Sophie.

"That's what Ben tells me when I sit and stew over things that are out of my control."

"Are you referring to our daughter in the Alps, Ellie, and our son about to become a rock star?" asked Ben.

"Exactly, honey!"

"I wish I was about to become a rock star, Dad!"

"Before I leave," said Sophie, "I'd like to hear you play, Andy."

"Really?"

"Certainly. I wasn't always an old woman. I remember feeling that the world was made for me and me alone. Being old doesn't mean you can't remember what love feels like, either. Being old means you are wiser. Should those feelings come back around, you don't let them slip away, especially if you let them slipped away once upon a time."

The doorbell rang, interrupting the conversation. A few seconds later, Sophie's words would be put to the test.

Chapter Thirty

Ben was stoking the fire while telling Ellie about entering Sophie's shop and hearing Perry Como singing behind the curtain. When he turned around, Andy was walking into the room with Henry.

"Henry!" Ben exclaimed. "We're so happy you could join us."

With Sophie's back to him, Henry didn't notice her at first. When he did, he was looking through the eyes of a young man at a beautiful, young girl with soft, brown eyes who swam like Esther Williams and laughed as freely as the wind. There was no need for introductions. Despite her cane, Sophie sprang from her chair as spryly as that young girl had done when diving into the river so long ago. There was no need for introductions. Despite the use of a cane, Sophie sprang from her chair as spryly as she once jumped off the big rock into the river. Even with the passing of time, when lives pick back up again, they start at the place where it all began.

So overwhelmed at finding Sophie sitting in front of the fire, casually talking and a part of Ben's life, Henry was speechless. That didn't matter. Sophie engulfed him in her arms and kept repeating his name over and over. She kissed his forehead, wiped away his tears, and kissed him again—this time, on the lips. It was spontaneous. It was obvious how overjoyed she was at seeing him. It was obvious that Henry felt the same. This was a side of Henry that Ben had never seen. We all have those sides of ourselves that are kept tucked away until life squeezes them out for all to see.

Henry kept her close to him. It was as if he didn't want to let her go, now that he'd found her again. He kept repeating how she was more beautiful than ever.

"And you are as handsome as ever, Henry. I can still see you coming down that pathway on horseback."

"We'd wander for hours through the fields. Remember that stream we found? We let the horse have a drink while we skipped stones and picked wildflowers."

"I remember you making me a necklace out of daisies, Henry. I saved that necklace—pressed it between the pages of a Longfellow book."

"You always did like poetry."

"I seem to recall a young man who liked writing poetry."

"Not Henry?"

"Yes, Ben, it was Henry," laughed Sophie, kissing her old friend once more.

"That was youth at its best."

"That was a young man impressing a young woman, Henry," Sophie replied. "I saved your poems, too."

"Do girls do that today?" asked Andy. "Save things like that?"

"With the Internet, I'd be afraid what girls might keep, Andy. They may be more apt to share it with the world," Ben remarked.

Noticing a look shared between the two still standing, Ellie suggested, "You both sit here on the sofa. Can I get you something to drink, Henry?"

"I'll have a glass of eggnog, Ellie. I may need more than one after this wonderful surprise."

Taking Sophie's hand, Henry led her to the sofa. They continued holding hands until Ellie returned with the eggnog and one for Andy as well. When they were settled, Ben stood, announcing the moment warranted a toast.

"I ask that you raise your glass as we honor loved ones found and old friendships rekindled. This truly is a Christmas we will never forget."

Glasses clinked as cheers echoed through the room—a room that had witnessed so many family gatherings. This gathering would likely be the most memorable. Sometimes life itself writes the best lines. Planning can get in the way of spontaneity.

The talk eventually came around to Henry asking how all of this had taken place. Ben tried simplifying the story. He went into detail when explaining how he and Andy had gone to Portsmouth after reading Sophie's letter addressed to Paul. Ben explained he hadn't confided in him simply because he didn't know what they'd discover in New Hampshire.

"So you're still sewing," Henry remarked.

"It's provided me a good life. I consider myself blessed to be able to do something I am so passionate about and call it work. You did the same, Ben told me. You worked your family's farm. I wasn't surprised."

"Farming made for an honest day's work. They were long days but good days."

"And you still have horses."

"I could never go without my horses, Sophie."

"You needn't explain. I remember how you cared for them. They were like your ... Oh, I'm rambling now. When you get old, you ramble."

"You'll never be old, Sophie. Growing old and acting old are two different things."

"I agree, Henry. When it's my time, toss me in the ocean. I've already spent a good share of my life in an institution. I'm not complaining. The orphanage became my home, but I've been too free for too long to be corralled back into four gray walls, no matter what color they paint them."

"I hear you. When it's my time, plant me in my garden."

"I miss the farmland."

"You have the ocean," replied Henry.

"It's nothing like the fields and pastures I grew up with. There's something to be said about working the land."

"That's what kept me here," said Henry. "Helen felt the same way."

"Benny told me about your beloved Helen. I am so sorry for your loss, Henry. You have my sympathy."

"Thank you. We had some good years together. Helen was a fine woman."

"I enjoyed learning how you opened your home to the children on Christmas Eve. They must have loved riding with Santa in his sleigh."

"I continue to hear from some who figured out I was Santa Claus. We did it together. Helen made cookies nonstop once Thanksgiving was over."

"Do you still get people asking you to take them on sleigh rides?" Sophie asked.

"After Helen died, I stopped. But life has a way of bringing things back around. I now limit how many I commit to."

"I do the same with my sewing lessons. I've figured out my time has value, especially to me."

"I feel the same way, Sophie."

It wasn't long before Ellie suggested they move into the dining room. While Sophie and Henry continued their conversation, Ben and Andy assisted Ellie in the kitchen.

Once they were seated, Ben asked Sophie if she'd say the blessing.

Sophie wasn't surprised that her tears weren't far away.

Standing, she put all of her thoughts into a simple yet poignant blessing.

"Let us be thankful for the will of God—for it is God's will that has brought us together on this night of all nights. To my Benny, my prayers have been answered. To Ellie and Andy, I thank you for welcoming me with open arms. To my dear Henry, you remain in my heart forever."

Glasses were raised. Henry pulled Sophie close and kissed her. It was another spontaneous moment. It was as if they were the only ones in the room.

Aware that all eyes were on the two, Ben simply said, "After such a beautiful toast, it's time to enjoy this festive dinner."

As the turkey platter was passed around the table, followed by bowls of squash and turnips from the garden, with crocks stuffed full of mashed potatoes and sweet potatoes and salads and all the trimmings waiting their turn, the conversation began again. Breads from handed-down family recipes and pickles and relishes made from produce grown out back were praised as twirling snowflakes kept falling to earth. It was a splendid gathering with such splendid people, and it would have been near impossible to top. But it happened with yet another knock at the door.

Chapter Thirty-One

At first the knocking was lost between Barbara Streisand and Andy Williams entertaining in the background. Then it was thought to be the wind. Ben decided to make sure. When he opened the door, no one was there. He was certain it had been the wind. But when he turned to go back inside, something caught his eye. It blended so well with the drifts about the doorway that he hadn't noticed it at first. The porch light made it stand out. It was shimmering. The small white box secured by a silver satin ribbon was nestled between potted trees and an old sleigh with old skates wrapped around it. There was no tag. There was no card. Picking up the gift, Ben hesitated. He thought about heading back inside and giving it to Ellie, who knew more about who was getting what and when, but he didn't. Instead, he opened the box and found an unmarked envelope. Putting the box down, Ben opened the envelope and took out a card. It was blank on the front. Standing under the light, it took Ben a few seconds to read what was written inside. The single short line stirred his curiosity:

Is there room this Christmas Eve for one more at the table?

The printing looked familiar. *It can't be,* thought Ben. Then he heard a one-word melody spoken by a little girl to her father, one that was ingrained in his soul.

"Daddy?"

It might as well have been a full philharmonic singing that word under the stars on this spectacular night. Ben stepped farther out on the porch. No one was there. He couldn't have imagined what he'd heard. The creaking of the swing hanging at the end of the porch caught his attention. Surely it must be the wind pushing it back and forth, so he ignored it.

In the shivering cold, another winter evening came to mind when Maggie was a freshman in high school. She'd made the basketball team. They were in the playoffs. It was down to the last seconds of the game. Maggie had a breakaway. If she scored, she'd win the game for her teammates. But her shot was wide. The other team got the rebound. They scored and won the trophy. Upperclassmen singled Maggie out as the reason for their loss. Hours later, Ben was worried. She wasn't home at the time she should have been even when considering it'd been a championship game. If only he'd insisted on her leaving with them. Wishing didn't help the situation. He decided to go look for her. When he stepped out onto the porch, he heard the swing creaking in the wind. He knew then (and he knew now) that when he turned his head, his little girl would be sitting there, waiting for him.

"Daddy!"

"Maggie? Maggie!"

That's all he could say as he scooped her up and hugged her "in a big bear hug, Daddy," just like she always asked him to do. It felt as if the whole world was smiling down on the rambling stone home, with its porch swing now occupied by a father and his daughter.

"I'm stunned. How did this happen?"

"Once I realized I wanted to be home for Christmas, even if only for a few days, it all fell into place."

"I have so much to tell you, Maggie. I don't know where to start."

"I have so much to tell you and Mom."

"Are you hungry?"

"I'm starving. Have I missed Mom's turkey and all her trimmings?

I kept thinking of her sweet potatoes and spice cake, all the way across the ocean."

"Every traditional holiday dish your mother makes is on the table, plus a few new ones, honey."

"Is Andy talking nonstop?"

"Your brother has grown up. He too has much to tell you."

"Is the tree in the front room? Does it reach the ceiling?"

"The tree's where it's always been. It's a beauty. We went to the woods in Henry's sleigh to find it."

"Henry? The old man who always helps you?"

"That's the one. He's here for dinner, along with another special guest."

"Who?"

"Let's go inside and find out."

"I love surprises, Dad."

"This Christmas has had its share."

"That's what Christmas is all about."

"It certainly is. Let's go surprise everyone!"

"I missed you, Dad."

"I missed you, my Maggie girl."

Most certainly the gasps in that dining room could have been heard near and far when Maggie made her entrance. Ellie couldn't get to her fast enough, with Andy right behind. Sophie knew who the beautiful young woman was, even before a word was spoken. It was written all over her son's face. Ben held back on telling Maggie that Sophie was her grandmother. After Ellie caught her breath, she made room for another place setting, and after Maggie checked out the tree, she joined everyone at the table. As she filled her plate, the conversation started back up again. Ben kept waiting for the right moment to introduce Sophie in depth. As it turned out, Henry was the one who provided the opportunity.

"Is the snow the same here as it is in the Alps?" he asked Maggie.

"There's not much difference, Henry. There's just more of it over there."

"I can't imagine getting a horse and sleigh through it," he replied.

"I forgot about that. You took us for sleigh rides when we were little!"

"Indeed I did."

"You missed the best sleigh ride," Andy told Maggie. "Henry took us into the woods for the tree."

"It's a perfect tree. It must have been fun going after it in a sleigh," remarked Maggie.

"That was just the beginning," Andy explained. "We went deeper into the woods, to an old summer camp."

Maggie picked right up on that. "A summer camp? Whose camp is it?"

"Remember I told you a few minutes ago how this Christmas has had its share of surprises, honey?"

"I remember, Dad."

"Well, along with you coming home, here's another big surprise. When I introduced you to Sophie, I didn't go far enough. You see . . ." Ben paused. "Sophie is my mother."

"Your mother?" Maggie sat straight up in her chair, looking at her father and then Sophie. "I don't understand, Dad. You had a mother—and a father. Andy and I had grandparents. We were there every Christmas—every birthday. We went for sleep-overs."

"Before your grandfather died, he handed me papers showing that I'd been adopted. That was the first I knew anything about it."

"Grandma died not saying a thing?"

"Dad told me she couldn't bring herself to tell me."

"What else did he say?" asked Maggie.

"Not much. He handed me a box of snowmen."

"Snowmen?"

Ellie spoke up. "Henry delivered your father, along with the snowmen, to your grandparents when he was a little boy on a Christmas Eve. Sophie made them. It was her way of staying connected with your father, although he never knew about them growing up."

"Don't tell me you took Dad by sleigh."

"Indeed I did!"

Maggie heard more and more of her father's story as bowls were passed and refilled and passed around again. While the conversation jumped from Henry and his sleigh to Maggie's experiences and Andy's forthcoming adventure, it always came back around to Ben and Sophie.

"I can't believe Grandma and Grandpa never told you, Dad—or that you, Sophie, were only hours away all these years," said Maggie.

"Oddly enough, your mother and I have gone that way most every fall on road trips."

"That's where you buy your antiques, isn't it, Dad?" asked Maggie.

"Yes, and all that other old stuff stored in the carriage house."

"Stuff has history attached to it," Maggie said. "I took an anthropology course one semester on individual groups coming together to form a unique sort of family. The orphanage and its summer camp sound like they have quite a history."

"They do indeed, Maggie." Henry cleared his throat. "That camp provided fun summers for the orphans. That's how I met Sophie. My parents ran a farm nearby. I'd bring fresh eggs down to the nuns to help them feed the boys."

"It was just boys?"

"I was older, Maggie," explained Sophie. "I'd lost my parents so in the summers I was brought in to help with the meals and to watch the younger ones."

"Ended up she did most of the cooking and sewing and mending and caring for the boys if they got sick."

"I didn't mind any of that, Henry. The nuns gave me a home and taught me skills from which I've been able to provide for myself."

"Sophie's a talented seamstress, honey," explained Ellie. "Your father and Andy visited her fabric shop in Portsmouth."

"I've thought I'd like to learn how to sew," Maggie said. "It's quite the trend over there with so many fabric shops tucked in and around the towns."

"Sewing fit me, Maggie. If you have any spare time while you're home, I'd love to show you the basics, but I wouldn't want to take you away from your family."

"You are family, Sophie," replied Maggie. "I'll find the time. And I'd love it, Henry, if you could take us to the summer camp by horse and sleigh."

"We're due for a little snow overnight," Henry remarked. "Could we fit it in tomorrow?"

"I have an idea," said Ellie. "You come by sleigh for breakfast, Henry. After we finish opening gifts, we can go to the woods, and when we return, you can stay for dinner. We'll make this Christmas an event!"

"Are you sure, Ellie?"

"I'm positive, Henry."

"We could do it the next day, Ellie. I know how much time you put into Christmas dinner," said Ben.

"I have the majority of it ready, honey. Going back there would be about getting in touch with everything this Christmas has come to represent."

"I can help in the kitchen," offered Sophie, "as long as there are no fish to fry!"

"No fish on the menu," laughed Ellie.

"We could do a little ice fishing on the way tomorrow."

"You're still a comedian, Henry."

"I had to try. I've never tasted better fish than what you cooked for the boys."

"It was the old wrought-iron fry pan. It kept the flavor from one batch to the next."

As times were figured out and a list started of what they'd need for their sleigh ride into the woods, the conversation flowed as if this family had been a family for as long as anyone could remember. When appetites were satisfied, Ellie suggested they move into the front room, adding, "I hope everyone likes spice cake."

"You never said there was spice cake," laughed Henry.

"It's the best! There's nothing like it in Paris!"

"Now we know why you came home," joked Andy.

With Maggie and Andy helping their mother, the table was cleared and trays with coffee and cake were brought into the front room. That's when Henry looked outside.

Chapter Thirty-Two

"You've got to be kidding!" Henry was standing by the window.

"What is it?" asked Ben.

"Most would see this as yet another beautiful winter's night. For those who see beyond the obvious, it is a magical winter's night. There's only one other time I remember seeing this—it was that Christmas Eve—when you were six."

After dimming the lights, Ben pulled the curtains back. His gasp brought the others. All became mesmerized by glistening stars enhanced by the shimmering moon, so full, so bright, and so very close to the earth.

"I've never seen anything like this," said Sophie in a whisper.

"It's as if the stars are polished in streaks of silver." Ellie wrapped herself up in Ben's arms, adding, "It's breathtaking!"

"It's amazing," said Maggie.

"With the moon so full, its brilliance reflects about the stars, making their radiance glitter ... like silver, as Ellie described," explained Henry.

"Oh, I see it, Henry. I see so much tonight." Sophie was in tears.

Henry reacted without hesitation. It was as if they were young again; as if they were free spirits with nothing on their minds but each other. Pulling his Sophie close, Henry kissed the top of her head. So much was obvious to those around them.

"This is why I came home, Andy," said Maggie, standing between her parents and brother. "This is what it's all about."

"Many are not as fortunate as we are tonight. For some, home is but a memory."

"That's true, Ellie. I know many who spend Christmas alone," said Sophie.

"Listen. Do you hear that?"

"Hear what, Ben?"

"The singing, Ellie. I hear carolers. They're out back, near the porch."

Everyone headed into the hallway. On their way to the door, they grabbed a sweater or jacket off a rack of odds 'n ends. A few minutes later they were outside, dressed in wools and tweeds and plaids, enjoying the singing of those passing by.

"Aren't we beauties?" Ellie joked.

"We're as beautiful as the moment!" exclaimed Sophie.

"I'd like to make a suggestion."

"Nothing's impossible. What is it, Henry?" asked Ben.

"You have to have faith in me on this one. What would you say if we go down to the summer camp ... tonight?"

Andy was the first to react. "Can I sit up front ?"

"Let's go back inside," said Ben. "There's too much at stake. It's too dangerous."

"If you're thinking about your old mother, don't, Benny. If Henry feels we can do it, then I'm all for it. I can't think of a more perfect time to go back there."

The discussion continued in the front room. "We can't go tonight, Henry."

"I repeat, Ben, you have to have faith in me. I've witnessed many a Christmas Eve, but only one other like this one."

"So because of the stars," Ellie said, "you are suggesting a risky adventure?"

"Point-blank, yes. It is because of the stars, Ellie."

"Going into the woods at night in the freezing cold is dangerous. I can't put any of us at risk."

"Believe me, Ben, when I tell you we will not be cold. Have faith when I say we will not be in danger. When we get there, I'll start the wood stove. There's plenty of wood inside. You forget I am the caretaker. Electricity is hooked up. The horses and sleigh are out in your barn. I have plenty of blankets. The stars will show us the way."

You could almost feel the energy from everyone thinking. Gone were plans and lists discussed earlier around the dining room table. Common sense had disappeared. A new suggestion, without reason and draped in doubt and fear, was taking shape. In the end, the wisdom of an old man was respected. Faith won the battle. Tree lights were unplugged. Cake and coffee were saved for later. A fire was extinguished. Out came thermoses for hot chocolate. Parkas, goose-down vests, long underwear and woolen mittens, hats, and scarves were gathered. The thought of going into the woods on a winter's night by horse and sleigh became the plan. It was put into action. Warmed not only by blankets, but by the anticipation that this night—this Christmas Eve—held unlimited joy for those able and willing to look beyond the obvious, they were on their way, with more surprises still to come.

Chapter Thirty-Three

HEADING INTO THE WOODS, THE STARS' splendor surpassed everyone's expectations. Despite the denseness of the trees, the path was lit up like a popcorn stand. Of course, the moon had a lot to do with it. The horses, galloping at full speed, slowed their pace as Henry maneuvered the sleigh around thickets and through piles of snow.

"Are you cold, Mom?" Ben asked.

"I'm fine, thanks to Maggie sharing blankets with me."

"Duck down!" yelled Henry. "Low-lying branches ahead!"

"How can he see them?" asked Maggie.

"He knows every inch of this trail," Sophie explained. "He'd ride his horse down to the camp most every other day. It was dapple gray. Her name was Molly."

"I like that name," Maggie said.

"She was a gentle horse. She had lots of patience with us."

"Clearing's ahead!" said Henry.

They were almost there. Sophie could tell. She became silent. Even though draped in shadows, she was able to recognize her surroundings. It was as if time had stood still. Sophie had only seen the woods in the winter once before. That was back when there was talk of closing the orphanage. This led to the nuns deciding to celebrate Christmas at the summer camp. That had been their last Christmas together. The orphanage closed a year later.

Coming back after so many years away, Sophie was startled by the beauty of familiar pine and cedar covered in glistening white. The boulders where she'd sit and play with little ones were covered in an icy glaze, making them look like giant marbles. She wondered if crayon markings remained on any of them. Benny loved his crayons. Sometimes, after she had him ready for bed, they'd sit outside and color and read his favorite books. There was no such thing as a TV set.

"We made it in record time," declared Henry. "No wind to fight tonight."

Once the sleigh came to a stop, Andy jumped off and grabbed hold of the reins. Ben helped Sophie down off the sleigh which took a bit of maneuvering with her cane. Clearing away the snowdrifts built up against the building, Henry opened the screen door to the bigger building and unlocked the main entrance. After he had the lights on, everyone followed.

Again Sophie fell silent. Going back to another time in one's life can do that. No one bothered her. Henry built the fire while Andy showed Maggie around. Ben and Ellie wiped down a table with a dish towel for the thermoses. Ellie even thought to bring paper cups and cookies.

Like the train station, this place—at night—with the moon reaching inside resembled a scene from a movie, only now it was Christmas Eve. The images were even more heartfelt. If they wanted to, they could envision a decorated tree towering in the corner with presents all around. If they wanted to, they could hear little voices praising the meaning of the season in song and witness the door opening and a man in a red velvet suit and a flowing cotton beard coming in with a sack full of gifts to the sea of children waiting—if they wanted to. And if they so desired, they could take in the aromas of breads and puddings just baked, as well as those of sugar cookies and spice cakes and chicken with plump dumplings drenched in homemade gravy, all made by a beautiful young woman who greeted Santa with a smile.

Sophie didn't have to imagine any of this. She was remembering that other Christmas down here in the woods. Henry was now by her side, his arm around her.

"Back then, I believed the decisions I made were the right ones. But coming back here as an old woman, I have my doubts. If I'd kept Benny, my life would have been filled with his growing up. I'd know his favorite colors and foods and views on issues and what he likes in his coffee, or if he likes coffee in the first place. If I'd only thought about the lives my decision would affect, that decision might have been different."

"What you're feeling is natural as one grows older, Sophie. We can second-guess ourselves all we want, but the truth is we do the best we can at the time. When Helen passed, I wallowed in guilt. Since then, I've come to realize that I did the best I could."

"From what you've told me and from what I've heard, you and Helen had a nice life."

"We did. She was a good woman. It's just..." Henry looked into Sophie's eyes. "It's just my heart was with someone else."

What had turned into an awkward moment was interrupted. Ben was calling for her from the kitchen.

"Benny's back in the kitchen, Henry!" said Sophie. "Come with me!"

Sophie's moment of doubt had passed. But the words spoken to her were not forgotten.

Walking in to where she and her boy had shared what seemed like endless summers brought more tears. Standing by the side door, Sophie listened as Ben explained to Maggie how he'd help make tarts full of jam.

"There was an old cupboard sitting here. That's where I'd roll the dough. After we cut it into different shapes, Mom would fill each one with jam."

"Do you remember going berry picking, Benny?" asked Sophie.

"No. There's so much I don't remember."

"You were very young."

"I try to remember. It comes in bits and pieces... like the Lincoln Logs and a storm that woke me up."

"You and your Lincoln Logs were inseparable."

"We found them packed away in my bedroom."

"I felt they belonged here."

"Just like your scraps of material?"

"Just like them, Benny."

"How many snowmen do you think you've sewn?" Ellie asked.

"I lost count a long time ago. It never occurred to me when I started that I'd keep on making them."

"I remember the tree was full of snowmen when Christmas was celebrated here."

"That was the first Christmas for the snowmen, Henry. Those were the only snowmen that were named."

"Why?" Henry asked.

"Sister Mary Beth wanted every orphan to have something uniquely theirs. She knew it would be the last Christmas at the orphanage."

"I remember how detailed they were."

"They had to be. Creating magic for children without families was daunting."

"From the reaction I saw, your efforts paid off. They played with their snowmen up until it was time to go."

"You were the perfect Santa Claus. Because you knew them, Henry, you were able to relate to them. Despite how hard we tried, I wonder if we came close to creating that feeling of a home."

"From the orphans I talked to, you were the reason we did, Sophie."

"I know I wasn't the reason for all the excitement when it was time to go."

"What do you mean?" Andy asked.

"When we were getting the kids back into the sleighs, we were surrounded by reindeer!"

"Were they really reindeer? Reindeer don't inhabit this part of the country," said Andy.

"Oh, they were reindeer! I saw them with my own eyes," said Henry.

"Had you ever seen them here before?" asked Ellie.

"No, and I've never seen them again."

"They were magnificent," explained Sophie. "They held themselves so proudly. Once the horses started moving, the reindeer did the same, and when the horses picked up speed, the reindeer picked up speed. They kept with us until we were out of the woods."

"They stayed back?"

"They disappeared, or it seemed as if they did. I couldn't tell. It was windy. The horses were kicking snow all over the place." After a pause, Sophie added, "It was a breathtaking sight. The children talked about it all Christmas Day."

The thought of reindeer on this night was wondrous indeed. Silence fell around that old building, but it didn't last. The faint sound of a piano playing *"Silver Bells"* seemed to come from nowhere. It became louder.

"I found some old LPs over here," said Andy. "They're all Christmas albums. And the record player works!" As old favorites played, the conversation picked back up.

"Remember Johnny, Sophie?" Henry asked. "He was the blind orphan who insisted on wearing suspenders even in the summertime."

"Oh, I do. I do. I haven't thought of him in years. There was one particular day when he showed up at the side door with a string of fish. He was with that tall kid named George who had freckles all over his face. George told me Johnny caught them all with a bamboo pole."

"A bamboo pole! Really?" Andy asked.

"As far as I was concerned, he did," replied Sophie.

"That's kind of like that kid Carl. He'd always say his parents were coming back for him."

"Did they, Henry?" asked Ellie.

"No, they never did. Carl passed away in his sleep, just before his thirteenth birthday. I think the poor kid died of a broken heart."

"If he had parents, why was he there?"

"There could have been any number of reasons, Maggie. They might not have been able to afford him, or there might have been an illness in the family," explained Sophie.

"Was it sad living there?" asked Andy.

"I never felt sad," said Sophie. "It's like anything else in life. You have the choice to look at it either way."

"True, Sophie," remarked Ellie. "At the hospital, I've seen people with the same diagnosis react so differently. Attitude is half the battle."

"That reminds me of those twins. What were their names, Sophie?" Henry asked.

"Alice and Annie. They were beautiful... very talented singers. That Christmas Eve they sang their hearts out."

"Why would someone give up twins?" questioned Maggie.

"I asked Sister Mary Beth one day. She told me there'd been six other children in the family. After the mother died unexpectedly, the father was unable to care for all eight, so he gave up the twins with the stipulation that they not be separated."

"Were they?" asked Ben.

"When the orphanage closed, they were still together. I don't know what happened once they were placed in foster care."

Flickering lights interrupted the conversation. After going outside to check the weather, Henry came back in and told the others that the wind was picking up. The horses were restless. "I think we'd better head home. The weather could turn for the worse on a dime."

Trusting Henry's instincts, they hurried. Ben took care of the fire while Henry hitched the horses up to the sleigh. Everyone else picked up and packed up, and when Henry returned, they were ready to go. After double-checking to make sure the place was secure, out they went. As Henry was locking the door, he heard gasps from the others in front of him. Turning around, he understood their surprise.

"It's like that other Christmas Eve," said Sophie. "What an astonishing sight."

"How many do you think there are?" asked Ben.

"More than the last time," answered Henry. "There have to be close to sixty."

"They really *are* reindeer!" exclaimed Andy. "How do they survive? Where do they come from?"

"There's no logical explanation. It has everything to do with this night. Anything else should be tossed aside. These magnificent reindeer on this marvelous night are reminders of the splendor all around us."

"What do you think they'd do if I approached them?" Andy asked.

"I tried last time. It's impossible to do," explained Henry.

"Did they attack? Retreat?"

"They moved faster than the wind, Andy."

"But they're reindeer," said Maggie.

"Yes," agreed Sophie. "And it's Christmas Eve."

That was the end of the discussion. Henry climbed onboard. Andy followed. After getting Sophie situated, and after he'd covered both she and Maggie in blankets, Ben snuggled close to Ellie.

"Quite the night, my love."

"As my mother said, it's Christmas Eve!"

After checking everyone a last time, Henry alerted the horses it was time to go. Of course, they knew that. They'd been ready for a while. Henry wasted no time. Once through the thicket, he let the horses go. Off they sprinted, hoofs kicking up snow, sending it swirling through the air. With so much snow flying and the wind howling, no one noticed the reindeer galloping right along beside them. The moment was deafening. There was so much power. There was so much might whirling up and under the sleigh. Faster and faster the horses zipped atop the snow. Faster and faster the reindeer soared as those wrapped up inside that sleigh became aware of their presence.

There was something about the moment; something that stirred a memory of another night when stars were sparkling and a little boy was huddled beside his mother. Ben and Sophie exchanged a glance. All she had to do was nod her head and Ben knew she too was remembering the last time the reindeer followed them home. That night, home was the orphanage, and although there was more than one sleigh, they were with other orphans in the lead. Henry was sitting where he was sitting this night. It was bitter cold. Sophie had pulled the blankets tightly around her boy. With his knitted toque almost covering his face, Benny was warm from head to toe. Even though the snow was flying in his face, when he squinted his eyes just so from underneath his hat, he could see the reindeer surrounding the sleigh in a fury. Benny was filled with wonder as he tugged at Sophie with a question. She pulled him closer. She drew an old quilt up and around, shielding them even more and making it easier to hear what he had to say.

Benny's question was a short one. "Are we going to fly with the reindeer?" he shouted as best he could.

"If you close your eyes and feel the wind and snow, and listen to your heart, then surely we are going to fly with the reindeer. Close your eyes, my little one, as we soar through this night with reindeer all around."

So now, many years later, with his heart full, Ben felt as if they were flying with the reindeer—the same feeling he'd sensed one wondrous evening longago. Surely they were up amongst the stars. Surely they were circling the moon. Although the little boy was now grown and the young girl who'd protected him was old, they closed their eyes with family near and again felt the wind and snow. They listened to their hearts singing. They felt the spirit of the season even stronger for this time they were truly mother and son, flying with the reindeer—as they did once upon a time.

Whipping past one field and then the next with the reindeer in the lead, the horses seemed to shift into a higher mode. Bounding forth in lightning speed, they passed the reindeer. They screeched through the pine and cedar groves. They leapt over snowdrifts with so much energy that, for those with full hearts, it felt as if that sleigh was off the ground. It felt as if it was above the earth and amongst those glittering stars, as snow fell and reindeer seemed to circle the moon right alongside them. Below, the earth seemed covered in muted greens and reds and blues, evoking a spirit of peace and goodwill. It would only last a moment, if indeed at all—just as peace and goodwill sometimes do.

In the blink of an eye, they were home.

Helping Sophie off the sleigh, Ben whispered, "It all came back to me. I remembered that other Christmas Eve, when we were in the sleigh with the reindeer all around and I asked if we'd be flying with them. You told me to close my eyes and listen to my heart. I did that again tonight. I listened to my heart."

"And what did you hear?"

"I heard you reassuring me, as you did tonight with just your nod."

"Sometimes words are not needed, Benny. They complicate the obvious."

WITH THE WIND SHIFTING, THE STARS were disappearing. The snow began falling a little harder as Henry said good night to Sophie at the front door.

"I don't want to leave you, Sophie. But from the looks of things, if I don't get going, I won't be going at all."

"Come for breakfast, Henry. We'll be back from Mass by eight. We'll make a day of it."

Anyone passing by might have thought the two lingering were youngsters. When the heart's involved, age is meaningless.

LATER WHEN SOPHIE WAS UPSTAIRS GETTING ready for bed, Maggie stopped by, asking if she had a moment.

"Please! Come in, Maggie."

"When I was a little girl, I'd stand in front of this window and watch for Santa Claus. I'd usually be half asleep on the bed when Dad would come in and carry me to my room. I thought about this window when traveling back today. I was surprised that it means so much to me now that I am older. Funny thing, it means even more, as does my mother's spice cake, and her breakfast after Mass, and the cookies on that plate and anything else my parents made sure they repeated each and every year. I wanted to be here for Christmas."

"I understand, Maggie. For all those years, I wanted to be home with my child for Christmas."

"I'm glad you're home, Grandma."

Moving closer to the window, with her nose against the glass just like it used to be, Maggie looked out past the stone fence, and way beyond the distant tree line blending into the heavens. "Even though I'm older, I still get excited."

"So do I, Maggie. It's Christmas!"

"I haven't told anyone, but I'm in a relationship ... a serious relationship," Maggie blurted out. "We're destined to be together. We know it. We feel it, but he's being transferred to the States. He's an interpreter. He goes where the State Department sends him. He told me not to worry, but I do."

"He sounds like a wise young man. Although you'll be apart, it will only be in miles."

"Have you always loved Henry?"

"What do you mean?"

"I see how you both look at each other."

"Henry has been my dearest friend for as long as I can remember."

"Your eyes light up when you look at him. That's how my heart feels."

Taking Maggie's hand, Sophie stood beside her, amazed how the young woman deciphered what years had kept secret. Of course Sophie was in love. She loved Henry for all eternity.

"Between you and me, Maggie, I believe some of us have but one true love. For me, that has always been Henry."

"Why didn't you marry?"

"Life is not a fairy tale. We don't always have the options we feel in our heart. Life plays its cards, and at the time, the deck may be stacked against you. However, life always has other decks to be played that we cannot see."

"It must have been so difficult realizing Henry was the one, while being apart and not knowing how he felt or not being able to see him, or even knowing if he was alive or not."

"I admit there were times when I wanted to go find him and blurt out, for all to hear, how I loved him and wanted to spend every moment of the rest of my life with him. But the next day, reality would kick in, and I'd put Henry back in my heart for only me to know."

"Being in love isn't easy, is it?"

"Being in love makes your world go around and your world stop. It makes you smile, and it makes you cry. It's not easy keeping it working, but when it works, it makes you whole."

"My parents have made it work. They've sacrificed for me and Andy yet saved time for each other. Now that I'm older, I realize what my parents have is respect for each other."

"That respect was apparent the minute I came through the front door. Those two have what we strive for, Maggie. I will keep you and your young man in my prayers. Fate is not within our control—just like the snow drifting by the window."

"Thank you for listening. I feel better."

"Love stories are all so different, Maggie. You and your young man are on the first chapter. Henry and I have yet to open our book."

"If eyes could speak, they'd say you and Henry are home."

Taking the young woman into her arms, the grandmother held her close in front of the window where a little girl had waited in anticipation. We don't always understand the curve balls thrown our way, but if we allow the rhythm to keep playing, our song will be sung.

A few minutes later as she was leaving, Maggie turned back around.

"My father seems at peace, Grandma. I never realized he wasn't until seeing him with you tonight. What a beautiful gift you've given him."

"It's a gift to be shared, Maggie, and that's the best gift of all."

DESPITE THE PERSISTENT WIND, THE HOUSE quieted down. With the dishes done and a few more gifts wrapped and placed under the tree, Ellie tiptoed up to bed. Pulling down the blankets, she crawled in next to Ben who was sound asleep. How she cherished lying next to the man whose warmth comforted her. The faint scent of shaving cream mingled with pine filled her senses as she gently moved her fingers through his hair, then reached her arm around and pulled him close. Nuzzling her face against the nape of his neck, she kissed him and then kissed him again and again. Ben stirred. Turning over, he brought his lips to hers. No words were spoken. True love comes unscripted as love stories often do.

Chapter Thirty-Four

One item was new on the Christmas breakfast menu. It was Sophie's jam tarts. Ellie had asked Sophie to make them. She wanted to surprise Ben, but that proved impossible. Their sweet aroma had drifted to every corner of the house by the time he made his way downstairs and into the kitchen.

"Where are they? I know they're here."

"You'll have to wait, Benny," teased Sophie, placing the tarts on a tin tray—obviously an antique. "Is this one of your New Hampshire finds? It reminds me of some old sets I've seen around Portsmouth."

"It is. There was something about the piece. It seemed to have a history."

"Just like you," teased Ellie.

"Are you implying I'm an antique? I seem to remember," Ben whispered, "you enjoyed this old guy a few hours ago."

Kissing him as she stirred eggs for French toast, Ellie whispered back, "I did—tremendously."

"Before today gets going, I want to tell you again how sorry I am for having pushed you away, honey."

"It's the tough times that have made us stronger." Brushing aside a few stray threads from his sweater, Ellie pulled him closer, adding, "I understand you had to make sense of it. That's how you work. I know that."

As she reached for the cinnamon, Ben took her hand in his and kissed each finger slowly . . . very slowly.

"I didn't know you cooked, Benny," joked Sophie as she covered the tarts with foil.

"He doesn't, Sophie. He prefers harassing the cook."

"I'll put him to work outside," Henry said, stepping into the kitchen. "I need some help with the horse," he added, with his arm around Sophie.

"You came by sleigh?"

"I came by cutter, Sophie. There's so much new snow."

"We found that out when we went to Mass," Ellie said. "The roads weren't plowed."

"They're still not in great shape, but it didn't matter. I had the back fields all to myself. I was thinking, Sophie. You and I could go for a ride in the cutter later. By then it should be even more spectacular out there."

"I'd like that, Henry," replied Sophie.

"You could go after we open gifts. You must have so much catching up to do," said Ben getting his first cup of coffee.

"Indeed we do," smiled Sophie, winking at Maggie who was standing in the doorway half asleep. That didn't matter. Maggie understood what Sophie was saying.

"Breakfast is about ready," announced Ellie, giving her daughter a hug. "You are the best present a mother could receive."

"What's that say for me?" Andy kidded, coming in from outside.

"It says you already know you are my other best present!"

While Ellie filled serving dishes and platters, brought in trays, and filled juice glasses, Maggie lit the candles and made sure her parents' favorite Bocelli music was playing in the background.

With snow lightly falling, the tree lights on, and a fire in the fireplace, another meal was shared by a family getting used to changes and new directions. This is what happens to families as one Christmas leads to another and children grow and loved ones pass, and surprises lead to more surprises.

"Now I understand why your French toast is a favorite, Ellie," said Sophie as she added another slice to her plate.

"The trick is in the bread," replied Ellie. "Your jam tarts add the perfect touch."

"They are so good, Grandma," stated Maggie. "I can see them in coffee houses. Wrapped up individually with a clever logo and a pitch, they'd be best sellers."

"They were, years back," said Henry. "I was thinking earlier, Sophie, how the boys would flock to that side door when they knew you were baking the tarts. That aroma spread over the camp like a blanket. Even on the hottest days they'd devour them right out of the oven. Isn't it funny how a simple tart stirs such memories? I smell molasses and I go right back to when I was a kid and my mother would be baking her molasses cookies."

"I did the same thing a few weeks ago," explained Maggie. "A bunch of us went out for a coffee. A few of the girls ordered the holiday blend, and as soon as we sat down, the smell of nutmeg made me think of being home for Christmas."

"It's proven that our senses are drivers of behavior."

"So true, Benny," said Sophie. "I watch people pick out fabric. They have to touch it. Some hold it up to the light. Some even smell the bolts."

"Your shop does have a particular scent to it," said Ben. "I noticed that when I walked inside."

"It has to be all the fabric and wooden shelves and antique hutches gathered in one small space. I don't notice it anymore."

"How many years have you been in that location, Sophie?"

"I've lost track, Henry."

"Would you ever move?"

"Why do you ask, Henry?"

"Just curious," he replied.

The conversation continued as they enjoyed the seasonal breakfast. Stories of days gone by and hopes for what lay ahead were shared as bowls and platters were passed around the table, just as they had been on many a Christmas morning.

After taking his last forkful of Ellie's quiche, Henry pushed his chair back. "That was the most delicious quiche I've ever tasted."

"Thank you, Henry. More coffee?"

"Just a touch, Ellie."

With wind chimes dancing and a horse resting and candles flickering, magic flowed through every inch of that home and barn and carriage house. When the plates were empty, thoughts turned to gifts waiting under the tree.

"I remember how excited I used to be," said Andy. "All night long, I was certain I heard reindeer on the roof."

"Maybe you did, Andy," joked Henry.

"Maybe it was you I heard, Henry."

"No matter how old you get, Andy, Christmas still holds surprises," said Ellie.

A few minutes later they were gathering in the front room. With the fire cracking and a fresh pot of coffee perking, more of those surprises were about to be unwrapped.

Chapter Thirty-Five

THE CUSTOM HAD ALWAYS BEEN THAT Andy and Maggie would sit on the bigger sofa and open their stockings. This year, that's where Sophie and Henry were sitting. They'd been apart for too many Christmases. So with Maggie sitting by the tree and Andy sitting on the floor next to her, everyone watched as they opened their stockings. It didn't matter to Ellie that they were adults. They'd forever be her children. At Christmas that meant Santa still filled their stockings, although Santa had to make a mad dash to a discount chain open twenty-four hours to be able to fill Maggie's. Actually Maggie had two this year. The other one was sitting on her bed in Paris.

"I hope you didn't put any underwear in here, Mom."

"I decided not to embarrass you, Andy, so I took the underwear out, as I did with your stocking, Maggie."

"Thanks, Mom. Underwear never was exciting," laughed Maggie.

"I remember in the orphanage we'd each get a stocking," reflected Sophie, "and every year there'd be an orange if we were lucky, some underwear and socks, one small toy, and a sharpened pencil. None of it was wrapped. In fact, any other gifts, if there were other gifts, were only wrapped in one sheet of white tissue paper. You could see right through it, but it didn't matter."

"We each have our memories," said Henry. "For me it will always be flying through the back fields with sleigh after sleigh full of children."

Once Andy and Maggie finished opening their stocking stuffers, Ellie cleared the way for the presents under the tree. She was always the one handing them out. This year was no exception, and there was one gift that couldn't wait.

"This is for you, Andy. It's from your father."

Just by Ellie's tone, everyone could tell they had to watch him rip open a very large box. Ben was intent as Andy pulled away layers of crumpled-up newspapers. Judging by his son's reaction, Ben knew he'd made the right decision.

"Take the guitar with you," said Ben, "and play it like you've never played before. Masters have touched that guitar. Now it's time for a new master to play it, in your own masterful way."

"But Dad, this is your guitar. It's been to Woodstock."

"It doesn't do any good to keep it in a box in my bedroom. It's time for the new generation of great guitarists to play their way into history—and that is you, Andy."

"Thanks, Dad! Thanks so much! I'll take good care of it. You were right, Mom. No matter how old you get, Christmas can still hold surprises!"

From out of the blue, Maggie started crying. She couldn't stop. No one but Sophie knew where the tears were coming from.

"I wasn't going to say anything," Maggie finally blurted. "But being here with all of you, I can't stop wishing he was here too."

"He?" asked Ben.

"His name is Teddy, Dad. I think I love him. I know I love him."

"Well, where is he?" asked Ben. "He can join us, Maggie. Call him up!"

"It's not that easy. He's in the middle of being transferred and has so many loose ends to wrap up. Sophie told me not to worry."

"Your grandmother is right, honey," Ellie said.

"I was going to tell you and Dad, Mom, but I didn't want to dampen your holiday. Sophie and I were talking, and it just came out."

"I'm happy you confided in your grandmother," Ellie remarked. "That's what grandparents are for."

"Where's Teddy from?" asked Ben. "What's he do? How long have you known him?"

Now sitting beside Maggie, Ellie reminded her, "Your dad is a collector of details, remember."

"That's true," said Ben, "especially when it comes to my daughter."

Maggie went into the details, telling how they'd met near Buckingham Palace. They both were with their own group of friends when it started to pour. They all ended up inside a little cafe where the two literally ran into each other.

"Teddy reminds me of you, Dad. He has a way about him. Within minutes, something clicked between us."

"Why don't you move back to the States?" asked Andy.

"It's not that easy. I can't up and leave all I've worked for."

"Companies in your field would fight to have you on board. You're good at what you do."

"Thanks, Dad, but I'm in the middle of getting our new eco-friendly cosmetics established throughout Europe."

"You've certainly done the networking."

"That's what Teddy says, Mom. He keeps telling me to get some feelers out and to watch Craigslist. I appreciate everyone's support. I feel as if a huge weight has been lifted off my shoulders."

"That's what this is all about, Maggie," replied Ben, looking at those gathered on Christmas morning.

"I know that, Dad. That's why I had to be here."

With Maggie feeling better, the attention turned to a large box sitting near Ben. It had his name on it.

In an instant, the paper was removed. Ripping his way through Scotch tape, Ben pulled the box open. Reaching inside, he found more tissue paper covering something that felt like a book. It turned out to be an album full of old glossy photos. Everyone gathered around. Sophie explained who was who and what they were doing.

"Here you are, Benny with Johnny, the blind boy, Bobby, and Lawrence. I remember that day. Before they went fishing, they built the sandbox you're playing in."

Ben studied every detail of the photo. "Bobby was in charge even back then," he laughed.

"Who's this sitting by himself, Mom?"

"That's Carl. I told you how he was certain his parents were coming back for him."

"He looks so sad."

"That's how I remember him looking all the time, Ben," Henry said. "Obviously these are the twins. Why am I standing between them all dressed up?" Ben asked.

"It was the annual summer celebration. We'd invite those who donated to the orphanage. Part of the event was a program. That's why you are dressed up. The twins were singing and they asked if you could stand with them. They were nervous."

"Henry! Is this Molly?" Maggie asked.

"Indeed that's my girl—such a gentle horse."

"You were quite a handsome, young man," Maggie added.

"Thinner too," joked Henry.

Ben went from one photo with his mother to another. "It looks like we had fun."

"We made the most of it, Benny."

"Is this you and Henry on Molly, Sophie?" Maggie asked.

"Yes. We were heading out for an afternoon ride."

"You're so beautiful Sophie."

"She still is, Maggie."

"Yes she is Henry—inside and out," smiled Maggie.

"Who's this, Mom? He's in a lot of what look like older photos with you."

"That's David. For a while, his mother did the cooking."

Ben couldn't believe he was looking at his father. His hands were sweaty. He felt tears welling up but he told himself to keep it together. Sophie didn't say any more about David. Ben understood. This was not the time. That would come. At least he had pictures instead of a blank slate. He put the photo back in the pile and kept searching.

He found a photo of Sophie with Sister Mary Beth. A few shots showed the dining room at the orphanage. One was at Christmas. The tables were set. The orphans were waiting for Santa.

"Am I in this one?"

"Those are your feet. You're standing behind me, scared to death of Santa."

"I remember that year," Henry chuckled. "You wouldn't have anything to do with me."

Maggie's cell interrupted the moment.

"Merry Christmas, honey," she said walking out of the room.

While waiting for her to return, Ben put the album back in the box. He'd go through the rest of the photos later. Maggie wasn't long. With the rest of the presents handed out, Ellie was overjoyed with Ben's gift of a Valentine weekend package in the city. Sophie was totally surprised by Ellie and Ben's gift—an offer to convert the other barn into an apartment. Ben even included a rough plan for a small fabric shop.

"So much to think about," she said. "I have my store and customers, my cat, my few friends."

"The offer is open. Think it over. I know you're an independent woman."

Ellie thanked Sophie several times for the little snowman. She hung it on the tree with the others.

After the rest of the gifts were opened, the clean-up began. Once the house was in order, Henry and Sophie readied for an adventure long overdue.

Chapter Thirty-Six

CHRISTMAS DINNER WOULD BE AROUND SIX o'clock so the two had all afternoon. Bundled up, they said their good-byes and headed out to the cutter. It had stopped snowing. The fields, trees, and hedges were sparkling. The wind had died down.

"Perfect conditions to go," stated Henry as he helped Sophie into the cutter.

"Does that mean we won't be seeing those reindeer?"

"Not today. They need a good storm."

"I like a good storm, too."

"I remember, Sophie."

Words weren't needed. Sophie understood what Henry was referring to. Sometimes when she was sewing, or walking to the market, or lying in bed, listening to the wind blow in from the ocean, she'd think about it. Although they'd only shared that one time, its memory never faded. Growing old doesn't mean you forget the passions of your life. After checking the horse, Henry climbed in next to her.

The snow was as fluffy as cotton batting. As the horse pulled the cutter through the fields and around fences, snow swirled up and over the landscape. The horse kept up the pace. He seemed to be enjoying this Christmas ride just as much as the two being pulled. Once beyond clusters of birch and maple, a covered bridge decorated with a Christmas wreath was in front of them. Neither Sophie nor Henry spoke. They were both aware they'd been this way before. Pulling back on the reins, Henry led them over the old structure.

"It looks the same, Henry."

"It's had some paint jobs and repairs underneath, but other than that, this bridge remains the same as when we last crossed on horseback."

"There can't be much traffic over it."

"That happens mostly in the fall, when people are out looking at the leaves."

"It must be breathtaking then."

"Not quite as breathtaking as it is in the winter. There's something to be said about the stillness. Maybe that's because the world is so busy."

"I told you before how I miss the fields and pastures, and now I know why. It is as you say, Henry. It is the stillness. I miss that. I do."

Once getting his footing back in the snow, the horse regained his speed. Henry let him go. The landscape was wide open for a bit, way back in where the snow and trees were untouched and the wind seemed to respect the solitude. Minutes after making their way up the last knoll, Sophie made the sighting. She didn't say a word. She couldn't. She tried, but every time, the words didn't come. How could they? What could be said about a thin line of smoke coming from a chimney nestled in a clearing surrounded by pine trees, other than what her heart was saying? Memories came at her as fast as the cutter was moving. As that thin line became thicker and Henry pulled back on the reins, the cabin came into view. It was as Sophie remembered. Even though it had been a blinding blizzard that brought them to this place so many years before, she remembered every detail: the three steps leading to the narrow front stoop, and the door, void of any windows, with its wooden doorknob. She still couldn't speak as Henry got out of the cutter and made his way to the horse.

"That other time I somehow found a place for the horse in that sheltered area over there in the trees. I bedded him down as best I could."

Sophie didn't hear one word of what Henry had said. She was making her own observations. "The steps are shoveled. There's a fire going inside. You've been here today, haven't you?"

"Years after that night, this place and all the land as far as the eye can see went up for sale. Helen was against my buying it, but that didn't stop me. She never knew why I wanted it. I'd come here every once in a while. It has a lot to do with the stillness... and you, Sophie. It has so much to do with you."

Beside her now, Henry pulled the blankets back and took hold of her cane. Leaning on Henry for strength, Sophie made her way out of the cutter. Steadying herself, she slowly climbed the small steps to the front door with its wooden knob. She remembered the two of them trying to get up the very same steps while battling a roaring wind and a stinging snowstorm, holding onto each other, fearful they'd be separated by nature's rage. But now, this time, sixty some years later, turning the knob, Henry led Sophie back to where they began.

"It still smells like a kerosene lamp and feathered quilts, Henry." That was Sophie's first impression. "The floor still creaks," she added.

"I haven't changed a thing. I couldn't. Whenever I spent time here, I could see us bursting through the front door, covered in white. I could hear you telling me not to worry about the nuns wondering where you were and when I would get you back. After a while, getting you home was the furthest thing from my mind."

"As soon as you carried me to that bed, nothing outside of here mattered."

With their coats and boots warming by the hearth, they sat at a table in front of one of the two windows.

"I don't remember there being a table, Henry. But then my mind wasn't on furniture."

"All that was here was the bed, the dresser, these few chairs, and this table."

Looking around, Sophie questioned how such a small and simple space could be so deeply ingrained in her memory. Of course all she had to do was look into Henry's eyes for the answer.

"It was never about this cabin, Sophie."

"I know, Henry. There was no fire burning that night, except for ours."

"And that fire has never been extinguished. The memory of making love to you remains as vivid today as it was when we were young and unaware how long it would be until we would return. I've loved you every second of every day that slipped through our fingers, Sophie."

Taking her hand, Henry led Sophie to the brass bed with a feather mattress where passions had exploded one January day leading into night. The windows were covered by worn curtains, the same curtains Sophie remembered when embraced in Henry's arms and the world stood still as she gave herself to him over and over. Now aged and wrinkled yet young in spirit and so in love, they sat on the edge of that bed and talked.

"I never wanted that night to end, Henry."

"Neither did I, Sophie. In some ways, it never has. So much happened so quickly back then. I tried to get to you, Sophie. The nuns told me to stay away. Once I learned of your situation with David and your plans to marry, I didn't know what to do. I made attempts to see you, but they wouldn't let me talk to you. When David was killed, I decided to make my move. That's when I bought this for you, but by then, you were gone. I couldn't reach you, Sophie. I tried, but I couldn't reach you."

Taking something out of his pocket, Henry handed it to Sophie. It was a small box, so worn that the words apparently inscribed on the top were illegible.

"Helen never saw it. I bought it for you. I kept it locked away, just as I kept my love for you locked away."

As Sophie opened the small box, Henry got down on one knee, right in that cabin in the woods.

"Oh, my! Henry! Henry," gasped Sophie, looking at a diamond ring sitting in the midst of a black velvet backdrop. "It is beautiful!"

"After that night, I had to put my thoughts on paper, so I wrote you a poem. You know me, Sophie. I don't say much." Henry reached into his back pocket and took out his wallet. "I've kept the poem tucked in here all this time."

Still on his knee, Henry unfolded the paper and read Sophie words written in the springtime of their lives.

Rage was at the window screaming to break through,
But nothing outside could match the rage when making love to you.

Inside that simple cabin, as the storm kept screaming all around,
Passions exploded again and again, as eternal love we found.

It was silent in that cabin as Henry folded the paper back up and put it inside his wallet. Then, taking Sophie's hands in his and bringing them to his lips, he kissed them gently. He simply said, "My darling Sophie, will you marry me?"

Before he could even reach for the diamond, Sophie replied. It wasn't the answer he was anticipating.

"I can't marry you, Henry. I can't."

"Don't worry Sophie. You can do whatever's needed at my place to open a fabric shop. You'll see how big my home is. I too have a barn we can renovate, if you prefer that for your shop. I like cats. We can visit New Hampshire whenever you'd like. I love you, Sophie. I want to spend the rest of my life with you."

"Oh, I can't. I can't." Standing now, Sophie slowly made her way to the door without her coat, without her boots. "I think we should leave. Ellie will need my help in the kitchen."

"Leave? Just like that, we leave, as if I never asked you to be my wife? You can't deny you love me. Tell me you don't love me."

She didn't want to, but she started to cry. "Please, Henry. I can't. I can't."

"Tell me, Sophie. Tell me that what I see in your eyes is not love. This is our time. Finally we will be together."

"But we can't be."

"Why? What aren't you telling me? Are you sick? Is there someone else?"

"Someone else? After all these years, how dare you ask me that! Someone else! There's never been anyone else but you, Henry."

"Tell me, Sophie! Tell me why you can't marry me."

With her hand on the doorknob, Sophie turned around. "I can't marry you, because I am not worthy of you."

"I don't understand."

"Believe what I am saying, Henry. I am not worthy of your love. I should not have come with you today. I knew you would bring me here. I wanted you to bring me here. So many times ... so many times when

I'd be alone, my mind would go back to our hours-minutes-seconds in this cabin. Whenever the wind blew or the snow flew up and around my bedroom window, I remembered lying here with you, Henry. I felt your arms holding me. You were right when you said in your poem that the storm outside was nothing like the passion inside these four walls. We were all that mattered. We were one. But I should have known. I should have stayed in New Hampshire. We can't go back, Henry. We can't pick up where we left off. We can't! We can't fit the pieces together, because the pieces aren't what you think they are!"

Taking hold of Sophie, Henry told her to calm down, but she kept on going.

"I've played this over in my mind so many times. I'd bounce it off walls lined with fabric, and every time, the answer came back the same. There's no other way to say this to you other than to simply say that you . . . oh, I can't! Take me back, Henry. Right now! Take me back!"

"Tell me what you have to say."

Something in Henry's tone calmed Sophie down. She stood for a moment, listening to the solitude. She realized once she spoke, everything would change. With a deep breath, she put into words what she'd kept in her heart.

"You—you, Henry—you are Ben's father. You are Ben's biological father, Henry."

Outside, a loose board around one of the windows knocking against the frame broke the silence. The cabin, once full of passion, was now full of confusion and questions.

"But what about David? You two were inseparable."

"David and I were best friends."

"But you were going to be married. You don't marry best friends."

"I didn't know what to do, Henry. When I told the nuns of my condition, they all—like you—assumed it was David. They called him in and wanted to know his intentions. David asked me to marry him out of concern. If I'd told them you were the father, I would have been sent away for good. You know what it was like back then. When David was killed, it made it easier for them to explain my absence, saying I was unable to handle losing him."

"Are you certain? You spent so much time with David."

"David and I never... we never... You are the only man I've ever been with, Henry. You are the only man I've ever loved."

"Then why did you keep this from me? Were you ever going to tell me?"

"It was a difficult time. I've explained how the nuns immediately assumed David was Ben's father. You and I, we had one night, Henry. I was young. I didn't know if it was just that—one night of passion—or if you loved me."

"You never asked me, Sophie."

"I was afraid of the answer, Henry. Being away, waiting for Ben to be born, gave me time to think. I'd decided to tell you about Ben when I returned, but by then things had changed for you, so I let it be. I tucked you away where only I knew of my love for you and went on. When I contracted polio, I felt the best thing I could do for Ben was to put him up for adoption. Never in my wildest dreams did I ever think that so many years later, you would ask me to marry you."

"But that night—that Christmas Eve when I took Ben from your arms and put him in the sleigh—right then—why didn't you tell me I was taking our son to live with strangers who'd raise him as their own? You should have told me Sophie. You should have told me I was taking our son! It was gut-wrenching leaving him with those people he'd call his parents. I thought of you every second. I thought I'd done my best for you while all along that was my boy—my only child—our child—back in that house in the arms of a woman he called mommy as she carried him up the stairs. My God, Sophie, you should have told me that night. We could have gone away—the three of us. We could have built a life together. I would have taken care of you and our son."

"I couldn't, Henry!"

"Why? We belonged together Sophie. We could have been a family!"

"No Henry. We could not have been a family. You were married to Helen."

Sophie grabbed her sweater and coat. She wanted to leave, but the horse interrupted her plans. He was making frantic sounds—so much so that Henry was outside in seconds. Sophie followed as fast as she could. She was in such a hurry that she forgot her cane. Henry found the horse in a panic. He'd trapped himself around some trees. Approaching him with calm reassurance, Henry unwound the reins caught in the frozen limbs and freed the horse. That's when he noticed Sophie. She'd fallen down the steps. She wasn't moving.

"Oh, no! I'm coming, Sophie. Please, God. Please. I love you, Sophie. I'm coming. I understand. I'm sorry, my Sophie! I understand!"

He couldn't rouse her. He felt her pulse. She was alive! Realizing he had to get her back inside, Henry found the strength to pick her up and carry her to the brass bed. Covering her with the quilts, Henry kept telling her that he loved her. He kept telling her not to leave him. Over and over he told her he understood.

"We have a child, my love. Please wake up, Sophie. Don't leave me. I understand why you couldn't tell me."

Her right hand moved, and then, so did the left. Opening her eyes, Sophie looked confused. Finding Henry beside her, the last half hour or so came right back at her. She started crying.

"Are you okay?" he asked. "Can you move your legs? Does your head ache?"

"I'm such an old fool to think I could make it anywhere without my cane. I want to leave, Henry. I want to leave right now. I'm sure you've had enough of me. I am so sorry for hurting you. Please. Please. I want to leave. It is best Ben never knows of this conversation."

"Oh, Sophie. Sophie. When I found you at the bottom of the stairs, I thought I might have lost you. I'm sorry for being so cold. I understand, Sophie. I do remember what it was like back then. I want to marry you, Sophie. We have a son! We are parents! I love you, my Sophie!"

Hearing his words echo about the cabin overwhelmed Henry. It only took seconds for the reality of what he'd said to sink in, even if that baby was a grown man. Henry considered himself lucky. He'd watched Ben grow. He'd been by his side all along. Learning he was Ben's father was icing on the cake. If he'd had cigars, he'd be handing them out. The emotion of the moment took hold.

As tears fell down his cheeks, Sophie felt his love even more.

Pulling him near, Sophie whispered between sighs, "I can't marry you, Henry."

"But you love me. I know you do. I told you, Sophie. I understand why you didn't tell me. I do. What matters is that we are together."

"It's not that, Henry."

"What is it, Sophie? Believe me, we will make it work."

"You don't understand."

"I do understand. Tell me what you mean!"

"The ring won't fit. My fingers are old. They've sewn for years."

"We'll take it back to the jeweler and get a different one."

It was quiet for a minute. Then they both started laughing.

"It's only been a good sixty years since you bought the ring!"

"The jeweler's been dead for thirty-some years. The store's been torn down for almost twenty. I couldn't take it back if I wanted to!"

"I love the ring, Henry."

"We can have it resized."

"We certainly can."

"Is that a yes?"

"In a strange, roundabout way, it is a yes. Yes, Henry, my dear, sweet poet, I will marry you!"

Taking Sophie in his arms, Henry kissed his bride. But it was too late. Sophie was in a laughing mood. So laugh they did, as they lay together once again on the old mattress. They talked about their son and how handsome and smart and perfect he was, just like any new parents do when counting toes and fingers, and checking how much hair their baby has, and figuring out who he looks like and smiles like, and wondering what he might be when he grows up.

"He is an exceptional architect," Sophie said.

"He is quite the guitarist, too."

"He has my dimple."

"Let's hope he doesn't have my hairline!"

The wind kicked up a bit more, bringing them back to that other time.

"Do you realize how amazing we are, Sophie?"

"In what way?"

"We shared but one time in this brass bed and we're still reeling from it!"

"We *are* amazing, Henry!"

"We really are!"

A few minutes went by.

"Amazing as we are, Henry, I have to roll over on my other side. I can't lie like this on my bad hip. I get spasms."

"That's fine, Sophie. I can't lie on my back. It makes it hard for me to breathe."

The mattress was a-flutter with the two trying to get situated.

"We can get separate beds, Henry. I can still tell you I love you before I go to sleep."

"We still are quite amazing."

"That will never change. I love you, Henry."

"I love you, my Sophie. My dear, dear Sophie."

They decided they'd tell Ben after dinner that the old man he'd grown so close to was his father. If all went well, they'd then announce they were getting married! An hour or so later, they were back in the cutter, on their way to Henry's. Sophie made him promise they'd return to the cabin over the years.

"We have a lifetime together!" said Henry.

"That we do, Henry, and aren't we the lucky ones?" replied Sophie, putting the small box in her pocket as the horse headed toward the covered bridge and beyond.

Once inside his rambling home with window boxes full of pine boughs and an oak door with a massive wreath, Henry showed Sophie around what would soon be her home, as well. The first thing that caught her eye was Henry's cat.

"She's a good girl, Sophie. She's been my best friend."

"My cat goes with me every day—from my home, to my shop and back. Something tells me they will get along nicely. She'll feel comfortable here, Henry."

"This house is a little older than Ben and Ellie's. Most of the stone homes in the area were built by the same stone master. You can see it's big enough and built in such a way that we could easily add a shop."

"I can see it here. I can feel it. I am so happy, Henry. I feel we have come full circle in a few hours. It's the way it was supposed to be."

"I believe that, Sophie. I want to shout for all to hear that I am a father—Ben's father—and the woman I've loved forever is going to be my wife! We are blessed. Only proves it's never too late for happiness."

Henry led Sophie through the rest of the house. She loved the built-in bookcases and the light coming into the oversized kitchen with its fireplace topped with an old mantel.

"It's narrow. It's the original mantel," said Henry. "That's how they built them back then. I've tried to keep anything original in good repair. There's so much history to all of it."

"Just like us," joked Sophie, looking out the window overlooking the barn and back fields. "It's so peaceful. It gets me in the mood to sew."

When the house tour was over, they headed back to their waiting family. This magical Christmas was far from over.

Chapter Thirty-Seven

With the women finishing dinner preparations, Ben and Andy went out to the barn with Henry. Andy brought along his new guitar. He and Ben took turns strumming. While Henry brushed and fed his horse, he looked at the two in a way he hadn't looked at them before.

"So how was your afternoon with Sophie?"

"It was more than I ever expected, Ben. She never ceases to amaze me."

Henry kept brushing the horse. There was so much he wanted to say, but this was not the time. *Soon enough,* he told himself.

It was dark a little after five when everyone gathered in the kitchen. While checking the roast, Ellie was the first to hear it. "Listen. It's coming from out front."

"I hear 'Silent Night.' It's the carolers again," said Ben.

The scurry began. Once coats were buttoned and scarves were in place, out they went. What they discovered left them speechless. It wasn't carolers at all. The voices were those of orphans who'd lived with Sophie at the orphanage. Most had spent their summers at the camp. All had received snowmen over the years from the snowman maker herself. All brought a few of the snowmen with them. With the moon shining as spectacularly as it had the night before, and with those little snowmen swaying in the wind, the moment was breathtaking. It was Bobby who stepped forward.

"Word spread quickly of your being here tonight, Sophie. We came to say thank you. Thank you for caring for us as if we truly were a family. You gave unselfishly each and every day. You cooked our fish. You tended to our wounds. You listened. You comforted. You kept us together over the years, through the gifts of your snowmen. We will never be able to repay you for what you gave to all of us standing here, and to those unable to be here. They too send their love."

Snow was falling, lightly, wondrously. It was quiet as Sophie stepped forward and spoke to those she remembered as little ones with skinned knees and bee stings and books to be read and pages to be colored and fish to fry.

"To say that you have filled my heart with what this season is about inadequately describes what I am feeling. Looking out, I see faces I remember as little kids running here and there and diving into the river and catching frogs. You truly were my family. We shared moments and laughs and sorrows that I've never forgotten. Whatever I did, I did because I cared. I cared when you were sad. I cared when you were afraid. As the years went by, I wanted to let you know I still cared. That's what the snowmen are about."

Holding her hands out for Ben and Henry to join her, Sophie continued. "I'm certain many of you will remember one particular little boy who was with me most of the time. This is Benny."

Sophie took hold of his hand and brought him next to her. "Benny has grown into a fine young man with a beautiful family of his own." Sophie paused to introduce Ellie, Maggie, and Andy.

"Because we are all family," she continued, "I'd like to share a secret with you, for that is what families do. Ben is my son, whom I love beyond words."

Cheers went up from those listening. Supporting each other is something else families do.

"I'm not finished yet," said Sophie, as she brought Henry closer to her on her other side.

"Many of you might remember Henry. He'd come down to the camp by horseback and bring us eggs from his family's farm. Well, just as I am overjoyed that you have taken time from your Christmas to come here, I have been overjoyed by Henry coming back into my life."

Sophie whispered something to Henry before continuing, "I have something more to share. I didn't know how we'd tell Benny, but God has shown me the way. This afternoon, Henry asked me to marry him. I said yes. Once a date has been set, all of you will be invited."

Cheers rose up again as congratulations to the happy couple were expressed. No one was happier than Ben, who grabbed hold of Sophie and Henry. Although there were people all around, the three spoke as if they were the only ones standing out there in the cold.

"I can't say I'm surprised! There was something I couldn't put my finger on. What a gift you've given me, Mom." Turning to Henry, Ben added. "Over the years I've gone to you for advice, for comfort, for assistance, and for the pleasure of your company, Henry. I think I've looked at you as a father figure for as long as I can remember."

Henry and Sophie shared a glance, speaking to each other through their eyes. They'd planned on waiting until after dinner, but plans many times fall short, especially when a meant-to-be moment is at hand and it's time to go for it or lose it.

Pulling Ben and Henry over toward the swing, Sophie spoke to her son, "Benny, there's more I must tell you. I'm sorry it has to be years later and out of the blue and I will understand if you ask me to leave. Believe me when I tell you if there'd been any other way I would have gone down that path, but life is not a fairy tale. Benny, my sweet Benny I must tell you—Henry is your father. Henry is your biological father. We were going to tell you later, but now seems to be the time. This seems to be where the path ends. I pray a new one begins tonight."

"But Henry…but what about David…but I…" Ben had to catch his breath. So much had changed in an instant. "But Henry, you…" Again Ben had to stop. "You never said a word. All those times we shared meals and worked side by side, and you never said one word. And David? What about David?"

"David was my friend, Benny. I never told Henry the truth until earlier today. It's a long story, Benny, and one I will share with you later this evening. I hope you can forgive me."

"Forgive you? Forgive you for what?"

"For everything, Benny."

Ben gestured for Ellie. He couldn't wait for her before answering Sophie.

"Why would I need to forgive you for giving me life, and caring for me, and making tough decisions in my better interest, and for planning to marry a man I've always loved as a father? To now find out he is my father confirms what I felt all along!"

"What do you mean, Ben?" asked Ellie, coming in on the tail end of the conversation.

"I've been told," Ben started to say, "I've been told that this old man here—my sidekick, my mentor—is my father, Ellie. Henry is my biological father. Henry is my dad, Ellie. He is my father."

"Oh, Ben!" Ellie grabbed hold of him. "You have the detail you wanted the most! I am so happy for the three of you. What an amazing gift!" Hugging Ben, Ellie added, "We have so much to be thankful for this Christmas! And I thought it was going to be a quiet one!"

Andy and Maggie couldn't stand being left out. When they heard that Henry was their grandfather, they were elated. Both embraced him and their father.

"So does that mean I get that sleigh of yours, Henry?"

"What's mine is yours when it's family, Andy!"

"I wish you happiness forever, Sophie. No one deserves such happiness more than you."

"Thank you, Maggie. I have a feeling there may be two impending weddings in this family."

"That seems out of the question," Maggie said. "So much is unsettled."

"And so much is out of our hands, my little one."

With old friends waiting to have a word with Sophie, family conversations were saved for later. Standing between Ben and Henry, Sophie greeted each and every orphan who came to her on the top step. Hugs and tears were shared. Old stories were rekindled. Many of the orphans looked the same; at least to Sophie they did. She knew every one of them. When Susan and Matt Bailey stood in front of Sophie, Ben made the introductions.

"I'm thankful your grandfather saved my letter, Matt."

"When we received Ben's email telling us he'd found you, we thought of Gramps. He would have been so happy for you."

"He was a very kind man."

"Ellie and Ben were kind to us after we lost everything in a fire," said Susan. "We were strangers, but that didn't stop them from coming."

Tugging on Ben's coat sleeve, Billy told Ben that Santa found their new home. "He brought us a kitten."

"What did you name your kitten?" asked Ben.

"His name is Benny—just like you."

"Benny the kitten! I like that, Billy."

"Benny has a new family," added Matt.

"Getting a family for Christmas is the best present of all," said Ben.

"We'd better get back. Benny's in a new home."

"We are too, Mommy."

"Yes, we are, Matt. We are very lucky."

"Take good care of Benny, boys," said Ben, giving them both a hug.

Thanking Susan and Matt for coming, Ben told them they'd see them soon.

Johnny was next. He still wore suspenders, although his pant size had greatly increased. George was without the freckles and seemed shorter but still had one eye bigger than the other. Only one of the twins was there. Annie told Sophie that her sister, Alice, had passed away some fifteen years earlier.

"She was a smoker, Sophie. No matter how hard she tried, she couldn't quit. It cost her both her singing career and her life."

Annie also told them she was performing in Las Vegas. She invited them out whenever they could get there. So many orphans stood in the twenty-degree weather to say thank you to Sophie and to wish the happy couple their best. Last in line was Bobby.

"I bring greetings to all of you from Sister Mary Beth. Although she is frail, the minute I speak of Sophie and Ben, she perks up. I too have my memories of you, Sophie. Thank you for giving me the foundation on which I've built my life. As Ben knows, I have a database with addresses of most every orphan who lived at the orphanage during your stay. I will wait to hear a wedding date and then get the word out for you."

Ben thanked Bobby for pulling off this surprise at such short notice.

"As I told you over the phone, Ben, there were others who wanted to come but couldn't get here for various reasons. We have a link on our website dedicated to Sophie. We've called it the Snowman Maker. Check it out and read what people have to say."

"Definitely, and we'll keep in touch with wedding details. She means it when she says you're all invited. You do realize, Bobby, that you all are her family."

"No doubt about that. If family is measured by sacrifices shared and unyielding support given despite the odds, then those of us called orphans really weren't orphans at all."

Ben and Ellie invited Bobby inside, but he declined, not because he didn't want to, but because it was Christmas. His family was waiting.

After standing on the porch and waving good-bye until each and every orphan was out of sight, Sophie and Henry joined their family in the kitchen. Breaking out the eggnog, Ben filled the etched glasses they called "the Christmas glasses" and offered a toast.

"To what has been a most spectacular Christmas, full of love and surprises and family from near and far; to Sophie and Henry, my dear, dear parents, may happiness bless you every day of your life together. You are proof that love is ageless. To my darling wife, thank you for staying by me through a dark time turned joyous. To my son, go make your mark as only you can. And to my daughter, embrace your journey, for while it may seem uncertain, there is a plan."

"Indeed there is," added Sophie.

Glasses clinking marked the moment. Soon potatoes were whipped and gravy made and bowls filled and placed around the table. Once everyone was seated, Ellie carried in the platter used through generations. She put it down in front of Ben. As was the custom, he would carve the roast. That was part of how Ben and Ellie celebrated Christmas in their home. Time ticked away as the holiday meal was enjoyed and conversation flowed. There was so much to discuss. Now, with a rather large wedding in the works, they talked about placing a tent in the field outside Henry's back door.

"I think that would work. There are plenty of places in the area for guests to stay." Henry paused, turning to Ben. "I'd like you to be my best man."

"And I'd like you to be my matron of honor, Ellie."

"We both accept." Ben smiled.

Ellie nodded. "I'll help you in any way I can, Sophie."

"Thank you, Ellie. If I seem a bit off, I'm still working through what took place on your front steps. Seeing all those faces brings back so many memories. I find it unbelievable that they'd give up part of their Christmas to share a moment with me."

"You were their mother, sister, aunt, and mentor growing up. You represented the head of their family, and through your snowmen, you've maintained that link," stated Ben. "I'm certain they went out of their way to be here. When you think about it, you went out of your way for each and every one of them."

"The timing was perfect," said Sophie. "Just when Henry and I didn't think we had many friends to invite to our wedding! Did you hear that? Our wedding! We're getting married, Henry! Your parents are getting married, Ben! What a Christmas this has been!"

Glasses were raised again, this time for the bride and groom. They lingered, enjoying the feast and the moment. Soon they'd again be scattered. That's why such moments should be cherished. They pass in a blink of an eye.

Ben was in the kitchen getting more ice cream for the dessert when he thought he heard a knock at the door. Dismissing it as the wind, he started to head back to those waiting, but something made him think he should make sure. Nothing would surprise him at this point. When he opened the door, the glow from the flickering strings of lights caught the edge of something sitting on the top step. It was a small, glittering Christmas bag with tissue paper overflowing the top. He knew what that meant. He knew that if he looked over toward the swing, he'd find a young man sitting there. Going over to him, Ben welcomed him to the family.

"Something tells me Maggie's told you about the meaning of this swing."

"Yes, sir. I've heard this is where the two of you have had some good talks."

"We have indeed. Maggie's going to be so happy that you came."

"I wanted to be with her on Christmas."

"I'll send Maggie out. Welcome to our family, Teddy, and please call me Ben."

As he walked back inside, Ben's thoughts went back to another moment spent sitting on that swing, only that time he was with Ellie after they'd learned they were to be parents. It was a totally new and frightening path for them but one they were overjoyed to be on.

"I never babysat," Ellie had said. "I've never been around a baby. Do you think I'll be a good mother? Do you think I'll know what to do?"

"I think that's where a mother's instinct comes into play, Ellie. You will be a marvelous mother."

"I wonder if it's a boy or a girl. It doesn't matter to me. Does it to you, Ben?"

"I haven't gotten that far, honey. I'm still thinking baby. We are going to have a baby!"

"If it's a girl, I'll French braid her hair. We can bake cookies and I'll sew her dresses and rock her in the old rocker, just as my mother did with me. If it's a boy, we can still bake cookies. Whatever this baby turns out to be, we will rock in that rocker overlooking the fields of this place that will be their home wherever they go."

When Maggie was born some seven months later, Ellie's maternal instinct kicked in, and Ben understood the meaning of the phrase "Daddy's little girl." Now he was on his way to tell his little girl that the other man in her life was sitting on the swing, waiting for her.

More than one path had begun this Christmas night. And one of those was years in the making. Sometimes while we plan and plot, there's something greater at play.

Chapter Thirty-Eight

When Ben told Maggie that there was someone at the door to see her, everyone in the front room knew who it was. When she opened the door, her reaction was heard throughout the house. About a half hour later, that door was heard again. As Ben was getting up to stoke the fire, Maggie walked back in the room with Teddy. Introductions were made, and then Teddy spoke. The interpreter clearly stated his intentions.

"I know you don't know me, Mr. Paquet, but I stand before you with good intentions as I ask for your daughter's hand in marriage. I love your daughter. I will be a good provider, a good listener and supporter. I will be her partner. I ask that you trust your daughter's instinct and give us your blessing."

Again the wind stirred and the chimes could be heard. This day, on high with emotion, was on overload.

"Please sit down, you two. I have to tell you, Teddy, you've already made a good impression. I have friends who receive emails from their daughters telling them they've eloped, so for you to come and ask me, I am grateful. My answer is simple. My answer is based on knowing my daughter. I've watched her evolve into a smart, young woman with common sense and a keen instinct for people. So, if Maggie is happy, I am happy. Welcome to the family, Teddy."

Everyone was eager to meet the young man who'd stolen Maggie's heart. They heard about his sister who was a dentist in rural Pennsylvania and his other sister who suffered from MS. His parents lived in Baltimore. His mother was a retired school principal. His father managed a chain of restaurants. Teddy would be starting his new position in New York at the end of January.

"You'll be able to find a position in the city, Maggie," Ellie said.

"Now that we know where Teddy will be going, I can get serious."

Ben was grateful they weren't picking a date yet. They were young. They had the gift of time. Henry and Sophie were narrowing down their October date. They were moving along like a freight train.

Later, when everyone was asleep, Ben and Ellie tiptoed down the back stairs to their other bedroom on the sun porch. While Ellie pulled down the sheets and added another blanket, Ben went quietly into the front room and turned the tree lights on. They'd be able to see them through the sun porch window. In the rush of the last few weeks, they hadn't had much time to enjoy the tree.

"Are you warm enough, Ellie?"

"Now that you're beside me, I am."

"Did you hear that, honey?"

"Hear what?"

"Silence. Except for the wind, the world has gone to sleep this Christmas night."

"At least in this house they're sleeping."

"Let's hope so."

"Ben?"

"Yes?"

"It's too quiet. Could you play me some of your music?"

Without saying a word, Ben was out of bed and back in a second. "How's that?"

"I love the Bee Gees."

"I know you do, Ellie."

"You know me, Ben. You get me. I love you, Ben."

"I love you, Ellie."

"We are so blessed."

"That we are. We are so blessed. Our daughter is engaged."

"You found your mother ... and your father."

"They might have been doing a little hanky-panky today in that cabin they talk about."

"I think they did years ago. Like we did whenever we had the chance."

"Like now?"

"Like now, Benny. Make love to me, my darling."

With Christmas lights twinkling, snowmen smiling, and a brilliant moon beaming, Ben pulled Ellie close. Bringing her lips to his, he whispered her name as passions soared and the two became one. The stars kept dancing as the Bee Gees kept singing. Ben's words rang true. Love is ageless.

Chapter Thirty-Nine

October arrived with all its glistening color. On this particular Saturday, happiness prevailed for a couple whose love had not only withstood the test of time but had grown deeper along the way. Everyone was gathered beside the old stone home that now included a fabric shop and a cat straight from Portsmouth. Maggie and Teddy were there. They'd arrived from New York late the night before. Maggie had thought she might not be able to get the time off from her new job, but Teddy kept telling her not to worry. The company that had hired Maggie was one of several cosmetic companies who'd fought to get her. They wanted to keep Maggie content. The couple still hadn't announced a date for their wedding. Ellie let it be known that she could be in New York to go wedding dress shopping whenever it'd work best for Maggie. She'd gone with Sophie and had a great time. Maggie had surprised them with tickets to a show.

Andy had been home for about a week. It was his first break from the tour, which continued to be a success. They were booked on Letterman for early December. He kept telling his father that it must be his guitar. Sophie asked him to play before and after the ceremony. Sophie had been living with Ben and Ellie since mid-July.

"You are a beautiful bride, Sophie. The dress is perfect," said Ellie, coming into the room at Henry's where Sophie was getting dressed. "You were right. You knew exactly what you wanted."

"It's the seamstress in me, Ellie. You learn how to sum up body shapes and idiosyncrasies early on and go from there. We all have flaws. The trick is to know how to hide them. The right dress can do that."

"I repeat—you are a beautiful bride."

"Thank you, Ellie. And thank you again for going to New York with me."

"That was my pleasure. Having Maggie with us was a plus."

A knock at the door interrupted them. "Can I come in and see the bride?"

"Please," said Sophie. "Come in, Benny."

"You're glowing. You are a stunning bride, Mom!"

"You don't think I've been alone too long? That I'm too set in my ways?"

"I believe that by marrying Henry, your life, which is a good life, will be enriched all the more. Ellie gives me purpose. Ellie is my other half, as Henry is yours."

"Thank you, Benny. Henry has forever been my other half, despite our being separated."

When she heard Andy playing the guitar, Ellie handed Sophie her bouquet of white and rust-colored mums snuggled about white roses. The accents of acorns and oak leaves had been Maggie's idea. She'd seen them when window-shopping in the city.

"Henry is waiting for you, Sophie," said Ellie, fussing over the mums.

"We've been waiting a lifetime, my dear," replied Sophie.

With Ellie going ahead of them, it was just the mother and son—like it used to be at the orphanage.

"You're not angry with me for all I've put you through?" Sophie asked Ben.

"I've told you before, and I'll tell you on your wedding day. It's because of how much you loved me that I am who I am today."

"I love you, Benny."

"I love you, Mom. Here we go."

"We had fun making our snowman families out in the snowstorms, didn't we, Benny?"

"We did."

"I didn't mean to wake you when I was cooking at the camp."

"I liked lying in bed, listening to you."

"Why?"

"You were always singing."

"Singing is good for the soul."

"Hearing you sing made me happy."

"Life is in the details."

"Living is in the details, Mom."

Blessed with a breathtakingly crisp Saturday, the ceremony was taking place outside amidst a cluster of maple trees glowing in glistening colors. If you stood under them and looked toward the north, the sunsets were amazing. When they reached the edge of the clearing, Andy changed the tone of the music. Everyone stood to honor the bride, who with her cane in one hand and the other on the arm of her son, walked toward the justice of the peace and Henry. As Sophie kept walking, she was overwhelmed by the rows and rows of smiling faces greeting her. Most shared the label of orphan with Sophie. Now they were there to share her day. Some caught her eye over others. Johnny's suspenders looked brand new. Arthur wasn't wearing his favorite blue shirt, and Carl, whose left leg had been amputated after being deployed to Korea for only a month, seemed to stand taller and straighter than the rest. Annie was on the end of an aisle, hanging on the arm of a young man who could have been her grandson. William—who insisted on being called William because he claimed he'd overheard a nun saying that was his birth father's name—looked to be quite well-off, judging by his three-piece tailored suit. Sophie didn't have to touch fabrics to know their quality. Finer fabrics had a certain way of hanging.

Most amazing to Sophie were the little snowmen being waved at her. There were so many of them. As she made her journey to the arm of her beloved Henry, she was reminded of the final day of the summer camp when she found herself surrounded by young eyes watching to see what her reaction would be when the doors were locked for the last time.

Today she did the same as she had long ago. With her shoulders back and a smile on her face, she moved ahead. Only this time, the love of her life was there to greet her. When love takes you in its arms, you know you've made it home.

"My beautiful Sophie," whispered Henry. "My beautiful bride."

Taking her hand, they went farther under the trees until Ben tapped Henry on the shoulder and whispered in his ear. Henry's expression alerted Sophie that something unscripted had occurred on their wedding day.

"Turn around, Sophie. There's someone here to see you."

"There are so many here to see us."

"But this guest is unexpected."

Sophie did as Henry suggested. The sunlight coming through the leaves blinded her for a second as it bounced off something shiny a few rows back and moving toward her. It turned out to be a wheelchair being pushed down the aisle of leaves and grass by Bobby. Slowly Sophie walked toward the nun who'd been both her friend and confidante.

It was Sister Mary Beth—the only person Sophie had confided in years back about Henry being Ben's father. Together they'd prayed that God would show her the way. Even though they'd lost contact over the years, it wasn't intentional. It rarely is. After giving Benny up for adoption, Sophie felt she had to go somewhere and make a new start. She'd stayed in touch with David's sister who had a friend in Portsmouth willing to hire Sophie. It was factory work, but Sophie didn't care. It was a start. But she never started. On her second day in Portsmouth, Sophie found herself inside a little fabric shop that happened to be for sale. She fell in love with every bolt of fabric and spool of thread in the place. It was obvious to the owner that the young woman with a cane was the perfect fit for his store, so perfect that he worked out the arrangements to make the sale possible. But even though Sophie had made Portsmouth her home, she never forgot Sister Mary Beth. In fact, it was just the opposite. The older Sophie grew, the more love and respect she felt for her friend, who was now in front of her and half asleep.

"Thank you for bringing her, Bobby. I'm numb with happiness."

"She wanted to be here, Sophie. She insisted."

"And I thought our day was perfect just a few minutes ago!"

"She's dozing, Sophie. If you talk directly to her, she will respond."

With Henry's help, Sophie edged in as close as she could. As a gentle breeze sifted through the foliage, one good friend spoke to another. "When I told you I was going to be a mother, you told me God had a plan. Even though I prayed with you, I didn't believe there was a plan. But I didn't know what else to do. I trusted you."

Sophie moved closer. "You were more than a nun to me. You were my best friend. You were with me through every labor pain and every struggle. You never turned your back when I told you my deepest secret. I love you, Sister Mary Beth. Thank you for joining Henry and me on our wedding day."

There was no reply. Bobby told Sophie to wait. A few minutes later, with her eyes still shut, Sister Mary Beth spoke, first with a slight smile and then with her hand obviously reaching for Sophie's. When Sophie tried taking hold, she found Sr. Mary Beth's hand curled up in a fist. When Sophie didn't take hold, Sister Mary Beth reacted. She opened her eyes. Sophie pulled Henry near. That bought a verbal response.

"I've prayed for this day, Sophie. Someone who brought light into the lives of so many deserves the same in her own life."

Taking hold of Sophie's hand, Sister Mary Beth opened her fist and handed something to her. "I've kept this all these years. Now, go. You two go get married and I'll be right here watching."

Before Sophie could reply, her friend was sleeping.

"She dozes off and on all day," explained Bobby. "That's the most I've heard her say in quite a while."

"Thank you again, Bobby, for everything you've done for me."

"There's no way we could ever repay you, Sophie. Now, as Sister Mary Beth said, you two go get married."

Turning around, Sophie looked at what Sister Mary Beth had put in her had. She didn't have to. She knew what it was. She'd held on to the rosary so tightly when she was in labor that she thought she'd broken it. But she hadn't. Instead, she'd lost track of it until now.

"Here's my 'something old,' Henry," said Sophie, showing him the rosary.

"I thought the 'something old' was you and me, honey."

"No, we are the 'something new.'"

"How so?"

"It's a new beginning."

"It certainly is, my Sophie."

With Ellie and Ben by their side, Sophie and Henry stood in front of the justice of the peace, who welcomed everyone.

"A mature love like Sophie and Henry's is the strongest love. It's the reason we are gathered here on this beautiful autumn day. Before we begin, I would like you to stand and give this adoring couple a round of applause. This is a joyous celebration. You all share a part in this union, which began so many years ago."

Applause rang out over the treetops and beyond the golden fields and pastures. Once quiet resumed, the vows were taken. The ring was given by a son to his father, and soon the couple who'd fallen in love while riding on horseback in their youthful years became one in the winter of their lives. The celebration extended into the night, and Sophie and Henry stayed until the last guest left.

Chapter Forty

Despite the blowing and drifting snow, the roads weren't bad. Traffic was moving right along. It was predicted that they'd get another foot of snow before morning. Ellie had called the station. Ben's train was on time.

From their phone conversation the night before, Ellie could tell Ben was determined to finalize any loose ends before leaving the city. This would be the last holiday season she'd be picking him up a few days before Christmas. Over the coming year he'd be working from home, not on designing new buildings and refurbishing old ones, but instead restoring antiques and primitives to their original state. Partners in Ben's firm were capable of stepping into his shoes. After all, he'd handpicked each and every one. He'd taught them professionalism, and he'd taught them perfection. He never taught style; that had to come with the package.

Ben made it clear that he'd be available for advice, but with Sophie and Henry nearby, he wanted to be there for them. He wanted to be a part of their lives. That was why he'd finished revamping the carriage house. He was ready to tackle all that stuff that was waiting for him. Ben's move was why Ellie would be retiring in March. It was a little earlier than she'd planned, but life has a way of changing things. Thinking you might retire is different than knowing when it's time. She'd started a list of things to do, like walking more, increasing the size of her garden, and helping Sophie in her shop. She was looking forward to taking sewing lessons. Sophie was starting them up in the spring.

"I haven't sewn in such a long time," Ellie explained to Sophie one evening when she and Ben joined the newlyweds for spaghetti.

"You still have it, Ellie. It's like riding a bike. You can't forget how to do it."

The couples took turns hosting Sunday dinners when Ben was home. They'd sit around the table talking—sometimes past ten.

Ellie lost count of how many times she'd waited for him in the same place she now stood. There was the Christmas when a three-day blizzard almost stopped everything in its tracks, including planes and trains and a certain car with two little ones eager to bring Daddy home before Santa Claus arrived. There was the year Maggie preferred being with her friends instead of going with Ellie to pick her father up. Ellie still remembered the look of disappointment in Ben's eyes when she'd told him. Fussing over her scarf and straightening her camel coat, she smiled, remembering the first year she'd picked him up. They couldn't wait to get back home. They never did have dinner that night. But it was last year that stood out, not because it was the most recent, but instead because she'd convinced herself that Ben was having an affair.

Checking arrivals, Ellie noted Ben's train was still on time. The hustle and bustle was deafening. Friends and family greeted people loaded down with packages. Others kept walking or talking on phones, tuned into their own worlds. Many were carrying babies. Some were dealing with tired children. There were so many people going so many places. A sudden scurrying alerted Ellie. Ben's train was approaching. She felt a renewed excitement, as another chapter in their lives was about to begin.

Catching a glimpse of him as he stepped off the train, Ellie smiled and waved. There was still something about him in the midst of all those strangers. For certain, he'd left his mark on the landscape. Now he'd be doing the same for old pieces of furniture made by artisans of long ago. With a hint of a beard and wearing the tweed jacket she felt brought out his deep brown eyes, Ben made his way to Ellie's side. Kissing her as he pulled her close, Ben told Ellie he was glad to be home.

"It's over," he said. "I packed up the last of it."

"How's that make you feel?"

"Satisfied with the job I did, and anxious to get on with it."

"You built that firm on your own, honey. I remember times when you'd stay up most of the night and then go back to work on a few hours sleep. You put your heart into everything you touched."

"That's because my name was on the line. People trusted me to do no less."

"I'm well aware of that, Ben. You never let anyone down."

"Speaking of not letting anyone down, Christmas is six days away. What's the plan?" he asked as they started out of the station.

"Maggie and Teddy won't be here until late Christmas Eve. Andy gets in Christmas Day but has to leave a few days before New Year's for Los Angeles. Since doing Letterman, the bookings are nonstop."

"As long as he keeps his head on his shoulders, that's all I ask. Any date set for the wedding?"

"No. Nothing yet. I expect we might be told while they are home."

"What about a tree?"

"Your mom and dad will be at our place in the morning."

"By sleigh?"

"Of course—the Christmas sleigh!"

"With this snow, it will be hard to pick one out."

"We did it last year."

"I hardly remember. I was in such a state, Ellie."

"Understandable, considering your life wasn't what you'd been led to believe."

"Now I can't imagine it any other way."

"We've certainly seen our share of twists in the road."

"That we have, Ellie."

"Can I ask you a question?"

"You have to ask?"

"I hope there's nothing for me in that bag of gifts you are carrying. Remember we agreed our weekend in the city was our gift?"

"I remember, but when you find something that's perfect for someone, you have to buy it."

"That's not fair, Ben. I didn't buy you a thing."

They had agreed there'd be no exchanging gifts after Ben had surprised Ellie with yet another extended weekend in New York right after Thanksgiving. He'd made reservations at the best restaurants. Their suite at the Plaza was perfect, as were their horse and buggy rides around the park. They saw as many Broadway shows as they could. Just as much fun—and maybe even more—was their time spent wandering and talking, holding hands, and getting lost in the crowd. With grueling schedules, Maggie and Ted joined them when they could.

Reaching the car, Ben asked if Ellie preferred that he drive.

"You look exhausted, Ben. I don't mind."

"How's traffic?"

"Not bad."

"Dinner ready, or should we stop?"

"Dinner's ready—your favorite. I set a table for us on the side porch."

"Aren't you the romantic!"

"I get it from you."

Reaching into the bag of gifts, Ben pulled out a small box with curly ribbon wrapped around it. "You have to open this."

"But honey, I have nothing for you."

"Please, Ellie. I can't wait."

Ben looked like a kid waiting to open his stocking. It's funny how that wonder never really goes away. Standing amidst the snow falling, Ellie pulled off the ribbon and slowly opened the box. Moving aside tissue paper, she peeked inside. The lights in the parking lot made it seem more like daytime, even if the wind was blowing those flakes every which way.

"Oh, Ben!"

"I had to, Ellie."

"How did you know?"

"I know how you are about little keepsakes that mark a moment."

"That's why I wanted this, but there was no time. We were already late."

It had been their last evening in New York. Maggie and Ted were with them. They were in one of those souvenir shops lining Times

Square before going to the theater. That's where Ben saw Ellie looking at the glass shelves full of trinkets. She'd picked up a plastic Statue of Liberty with the word CHRISTMAS and the year embossed on its front. There had to have been dozens of them lined up, right alongside ashtrays and shot glasses. When Ben told them they had to hurry, she put the statue down.

"You were right, Ben. This is the perfect gift. I'll treasure it forever."

On the way home, Ben fell asleep. Getting off at their exit, Ellie paused for oncoming traffic. With the signal light ticking in rhythm to windshield wipers humming and snow falling, Ellie looked over at Ben who was curled up with his head against the window. Tears came from nowhere.

"Merry Christmas, my love," she whispered in the silence of a winter's night. "Merry Christmas, and welcome home."

Barbara Briggs Ward is a writer who lives in Ogdensburg, New York. She is the author of the award-winning Christmas story, *The Reindeer Keeper,* represented by Bergman Entertainment, Los Angeles, for option of film rights and chosen by Yahoo's Christmas Book Club Group as their December, 2012 Book of the Month. Her short stories and articles have appeared in the Chicken Soup for the Soul book, *Christmas Magic,* the Chicken Soup for the Soul book, *Family Caregivers, Ladies' Home Journal, The Crafts Report, Highlights for Children,* and is a regular contributor to www.boomer-living.com. Her projects include creator of the Snarly Sally book series. She has been a featured author on Mountain Lake PBS in Plattsburgh, New York and at Target book festivals in Boston and New York City. Barbara invites you to visit www.barbarabriggsward.com.

Suzanne Langelier-Lebeda is an award-winning graphic designer/illustrator. She earned national awards for art and publication design as a coordinator of publications at the State University of Potsdam. Her projects have included illustrations for the National Park Service Cumberland Island National Seashore Visitors Center, Georgia; Renee Fleming Benefit Concert materials, New York City; *Adirondack Life* and *Country Living Gardener* magazines; St. Lawrence University; Clarkson University; and graphic design for the permanent exhibit on History and Traditions at SUNY Potsdam. She is a member of the Adirondack Artists' Guild in Saranac Lake, New York. In her fine artwork she primarily concentrates on contemplative nature studies that explore intimations in nature by integrating watercolor, drawing, writing, and digital photography. Suzanne invites you to visit www.suzannelebeda.com.

Made in the USA
Middletown, DE
30 December 2021